Just three little words.

He hunkered down in front of Laura, and she hugged him around the neck before they exchanged kisses.

"I love you, Daddy."

"Love you, too, baby."

He straightened, and his brown-eyed gaze bore into Nancie. She held her breath, waiting for him to say he loved her, too.

But he didn't.

"Good night," he said.

" 'Night, Wren." With that Nancie led Laura down the walkway and to her car. She felt oddly disappointed, but immediately told herself that was nonsense. She didn't want Wren to love her. She didn't love him.

Once in the car, she pulled away from the curb and refused to look back.

ANDREA BOESHAAR was born and raised in Milwaukee, Wisconsin. Married for twenty years, she and her husband, Daniel, have three adult sons. Andrea has been writing for over thirteen years, but writing exclusively for the Christian market for six. Writing is something she loves to share, as well as help others develop. Andrea quit her job to stay home, take care of her family, and write.

HEARTSONG PRESENTS

Books under the pen name Andrea Shaar
HP79—An Unwilling Warrior

Books by Andrea Boeshaar
HP188—An Uncertain Heart
HP238—Annie's Song
HP270—Promise Me Forever
HP279—An Unexpected Love
HP301—Second Time Around
HP342—The Haven of Rest
HP359—An Undaunted Faith
HP381—Southern Sympathies

Castle in the Clouds

Andrea Boeshaar

Heartsong Presents

To the glory of the greatest hero, in the best romance ever, the Lord and Savior, Jesus Christ.

And to my husband, Daniel, who often waits in the wings, holds my kite strings, and never lets go.

A note from the author:
I love to hear from my readers! You may correspond with me by writing:
Andrea Boeshaar
Author Relations
PO Box 719
Uhrichsville, OH 44683

ISBN 1-58660-065-6

CASTLE IN THE CLOUDS

Cover illustration by Kay Salem

PRINTED IN THE U.S.A.

one

Wren Nickelson's index fingers pecked laboriously at the electric typewriter keys:

"You're crazy to even think about buying this ancient, falling down, gutted-out hunk of rock!" Joe told his twin brother, George, as the two of them ambled through the eerie gray-stone castle.

"The price is right," George replied cheerfully. "The state of Saxony is only asking one German mark." He chuckled. "That's just over half a U.S. dollar. For a castle! My very own castle!"

Joe threw him a pathetic look. "Such a deal. It'll cost seven million in repairs!"

George shrugged nonchalantly. His brother didn't know that money was no object. He had more than enough in his Swiss bank account. . . .

Wren sat back and gazed at the last sentence he'd written. Running a hand through his dark brown hair, he wondered if the Swiss bank account idea was too farfetched. *Guess it is,* he decided. *Better make that seven million available through grants or. . .or God's provision. Yes! That's it!*

With renewed vigor he grabbed the bottle of correction fluid, painted over his errors, and blew on the page until it dried. Then he reworked the initial chapter of his very first novel. After another hour had passed, he decided there wasn't much else he wanted to change at this point. He liked his characters, George and Joe. Rather, he liked their names. Simple. Common. Strong. Not at all resembling his own name—Wren. Unique, yes. But odd. Disappointing.

His name was Welsh and meant "ruler," and his mom,

5

bless her heart, had determined upon his birth that her beloved son would someday be a great leader. Instead, he'd become a mail carrier and aspiring novelist who couldn't afford a computer just yet. But worst of all, he'd become a broken man whose wife had divorced him more than a year ago, stating that she couldn't live with him or his "religion."

Wren didn't completely understand Nancie's reasoning for ending their twelve-year marriage. What he did know, however, was that the woman who meant almost everything to him didn't love him anymore, a fact that still crimped his heart and seared his soul. Now he was a court-ordered weekend dad, and for the longest time, he had felt lonely and depressed over the divorce ruling. But amazingly enough, without Nancie and his two daughters—Alexa and Laura—around, he suddenly found the time to do the very thing he used to only dream about doing.

Write.

It was like God's blessing of encouragement, sent from heaven just for him. He'd lost so much—his house, his family—but the Lord had given him an outlet for his emotional pain. And for the past four months a Monday evening creative writing class and imaginary characters had kept him company. He was only too glad that Risa had suggested they take the class together. He probably wouldn't have done it on his own. But she was rapidly becoming a good friend, and that congenial push was all he had needed.

Maybe he'd even be able to buy that computer soon.

Wren shook himself from his reverie and glanced at his wristwatch. It was past midnight, and he had to be at the post office by seven A.M. He stood, stretched, and decided to call it a night.

❧

Nancie Nickelson gently shook her two girls awake. "Time to get up. Mommy has to go to work."

Alexa, eleven years old, and Laura, age seven, groaned. After all, it was six in the morning.

Stifling a yawn of her own, Nancie walked across the girls' bedroom and opened the shades. Slivers of early-morning May sunlight quickly cut the darkness.

"Is it gonna be a nice day today, Mumma?" Laura asked, brushing blond bangs out of her eyes. "Maybe Mrs. Baird will take us to the park again."

"Yes, maybe she will." Nancie smiled at her youngest, recalling the fun Ruth Baird, the girls' baby-sitter, had described to her yesterday when she'd picked up the girls. Having three children of her own, Ruth was the perfect day care provider for the Nickelson girls. And Nancie ought to know: She'd been through half a dozen baby-sitters in the past eighteen months before finding Ruth at the end of March.

"Come on now, girls. Get up and get dressed. Everything's ready for you—even breakfast."

Nancie left their bedroom, reflecting on her hectic lifestyle. Laying out clothes and loading backpacks were tasks she ordinarily did each night after Alexa and Laura went to bed. Next she routinely would wash dishes and tidy up their compact two-bedroom apartment before pouring herself into homework and studying for classes at the college she attended on weekends. When her fatigued body refused to accommodate her pace any longer, she collapsed into bed.

After five or six hours of sleep, Nancie would force herself out of bed before sunrise and begin a new day, which would be just as busy as its predecessor. She started off each day by preparing coffee for herself and toast and cereal for her daughters. By seven o'clock the rush was on, first to Ruth's house, just a few blocks away—her daughters walked to school from there—then to the sales department of a large manufacturing company, where Nancie had managed to land a terrific job.

And this morning promised to be as hectic as any other.

"Don't forget, your father is coming to pick you two up this afternoon," she reminded her daughters after they arrived at Ruth's.

"Aren't you ever gonna be done with school?" eleven-year-old Alexa asked, her deep brown eyes glowering with something akin to resentment.

"I've got two years left to go. You know that."

"Seems like forever," the girl groused before turning and entering the Bairds' home.

"Good-bye, Alexa," Nancie called after her.

There was no reply, and Nancie felt terrible.

"She'll be all right," Ruth assured her. She stood at the front door with a baby on her hip. Wisps of light brown hair blew onto her cheek, and with her free hand, she brushed them back off her face.

"This has been happening more and more often," Nancie confided. "Last night Alexa and I had a full-fledged argument. Sometimes I feel like she hates me." Sudden anger rose inside Nancie as she wondered what Wren was telling the girls. Would he stoop so low as to poison their minds against her? Nancie couldn't be sure. She knew her ex-husband was a Christian and that he wasn't ambitious by any stretch of the imagination. But Wren loved his daughters, and Nancie had an inkling he might be working behind her back, trying to get custody of them.

"Nancie, divorce is always hard on kids," Ruth said gently. "Alexa and Laura only get to see their father on weekends, and it's hard for them to get bounced between you two."

"They're not being 'bounced,' " she said, sounding defensive to her own ears. She toned down her voice. "It's a schedule like any other, and children are very adaptable. As for Wren, I think he's up to something."

"Like what?" Ruth tipped her head curiously.

"Like. . .oh, never mind," Nancie said hotly. "You're on his side. You Christians all stick together."

"That's not true. I'm not on anyone's side. But I care about the girls."

Ignoring the comment, Nancie gathered Laura into her arms and kissed her good-bye. She couldn't dally any longer—she had to get to work. And tomorrow she was supposed to give a speech on women's rights for her sociology class, so she'd have to do some last-minute preparation on her lunch break. It was going to be another long and busy day. She didn't need to start it off this way.

"I love you. You be good for Mrs. Baird," Nancie told Laura, squelching the hurt caused by Alexa's aloofness.

"I will," the child promised sweetly.

Straightening, she smiled at the woman whose lifestyle seemed so opposite to her own. But Nancie had made her decision, and being a "domestic engineer" would never suit her again. Actually, it had never suited her. She'd always wanted more out of life than staying home and raising kids afforded. Now she had it. And in a couple of years, after she finished college, she reminded herself, she'd have it all.

"Bye, Ruth. Thanks."

"Have a good day."

With a parting nod, Nancie pivoted and walked back to her car. Climbing inside, she started thinking about Alexa's recent antagonistic behavior and then wondered why Wren didn't just say something if he wanted custody—not that she'd give in to the request, of course. But he could at least quit being such a coward and tell her face-to-face what was on his mind. But no, instead he used sneaky, dirty, underhanded tricks to drive a wedge between a mother and her daughter.

"Well, Wren, you're going to have a fight on your hands if you're trying to take my girls away from me," Nancie muttered angrily, pulling away from the curb. "A fight like you've never known. . ."

&

With two leather satchels strapped across his chest, Wren

walked his mail route and thought about his novel, *Castle in the Clouds*. He hadn't told another soul he was writing it. The project was his secret outlet, much like a very private diary. It gave him a welcome sense of purpose, and amazingly, he felt as though his heart was on the mend. Maybe one day he would even get the book published!

Smiling to himself, he mulled over his plot. The story line wasn't at all complex. A divorced man, George, buys a castle in Germany, fixes it up, then kidnaps his ex-wife, Nan. Alone together within the confines of the castle walls, she has no choice but to face the fact that she's always been in love with him. The divorce was a horrible mistake. An American missionary, the pastor of a church near the castle, is summoned, and George and Nan are remarried. They send for their two adorable daughters, who had been with a baby-sitter in America. . .and then they discover the treasure buried within one of the castle's walls. However, George's evil twin brother, Joe, devises a scheme to steal it away from the happy couple and their young daughters.

Wren continued on his way, still pondering his great American novel until he finally finished his route. Once back at the post office, he punched out and then headed to pick up Alexa and Laura from the baby-sitter's house.

Wren couldn't say he minded the girls staying at the Bairds' home while Nancie worked. Ruth and her husband, Max, were wonderful Christian people. So far Nancie hadn't complained about their "religion" and Wren hoped she never would.

He pulled his 1985 Crown Victoria station wagon alongside the curb in front of the Bairds' red brick house. Climbing out from behind the wheel, he headed for the driveway. Halfway there, he spotted Ruth and five kids—two of them his—coming down the sidewalk.

"Daddy!" Laura cried, running toward him.

Right behind her, Alexa smiled and waved.

Smiling broadly, Wren felt like he was in a Kodak commercial, celebrating the moments of his life. He wished he could forever etch in his memory the delighted expressions on his daughters' faces as they raced to greet him. As he opened his arms wide, the girls rushed into his embrace.

"Hi, Daddy!" Laura said, hugging him around the waist.

"Hi, baby." Wren placed a kiss on her blond head. Her hair felt feathery soft against his lips and smelled like sunshine.

"We're just getting home from school," Alexa informed him as Wren kissed her forehead.

"Guess I've got good timing today, huh?"

"Can we have pizza tonight?" his youngest asked.

Wren chuckled. "Sure."

By now, Ruth and her brood had reached them. "Happy Friday, Wren."

"Thanks. Same to you."

Ruth instructed Alexa and Laura to wait over by their father's car. "I think you should know," she began, once the girls were out of earshot, "that Nancie was a little upset this morning. She and Alexa still aren't getting along well."

"Hm. . ."

"Nancie thinks you're up to something."

Wren blew out a weary sigh. "Well, thanks for the warning. I'll try to talk with her Sunday evening, but I doubt it'll do any good."

"We'll be praying for you."

"I appreciate it."

Ruth's baby began squirming in his stroller, wailing for freedom.

"How much do I owe you this week?" Wren asked.

He settled up with her, then pocketed his wallet. As he strode toward his dilapidated vehicle, the irony struck him. Nancie got "liberated" and he got stuck with the day care bill. Perhaps he ought to talk to her about picking up the tab each week. Or even every other week. Wren grimaced at the thought of an encounter with his ex-wife. He wouldn't win. He never did.

Sliding in behind the wheel of the station wagon, he wondered what his character George would do if Nan stuck him with the sitter's bill week after week. Wren smirked. George wouldn't take it for a minute. He'd confront Nan and tell her that she had to at least pay half. George wouldn't let a woman push him around. George was a man's man.

"Dad, tell Laura to move over," Alexa whined from the backseat.

Wren twisted around to settle the matter.

"I hate little sisters," Alexa spat. "I hate everything."

"Even pizza?"

Wren couldn't help the easy quip, but it worked. After a roll of her eyes, Alexa smiled.

"Okay, who's hungry?" he asked, slipping the key into the car's ignition.

"I am!" Laura cried.

"Me, too," Alexa admitted grudgingly.

"Well, so am I." Wren grinned and stepped on the accelerator. "Let's go find some food!"

two

"Mary Wollstonecraft, an eighteenth-century feminist. Lucretia Coffin Mott, Elizabeth Cady Stanton—both pioneer activists in women's rights. Betty Friedan, the founder of the NOW organization. . ." Nancie paused, hoping for a dramatic effect. "What would these leading feminists think of us today? Women are still slaves in their own homes. Slaves to piles of laundry, dirty diapers, and their husbands' smelly socks. . ."

Nancie paused again as an image of Ruth Baird flitted through her mind. What would she do if she didn't have Ruth watching her daughters? Her conscience pricked her. Ruth, after all, said she liked staying home and taking care of her kids—and Alexa and Laura, too. She really ought to be fair to everyone.

Taking the pencil from behind her ear, Nancie added the word "some" and began practicing her speech from where she'd left off. "Some women are still slaves in their own homes. . . ."

After she rehearsed her speech several more times, she finally felt confident enough to give it in class the next day. And then she'd get her semester grade. School would be over for the summer. Nancie sighed with relief. She needed the break. Working full-time and carrying a twelve-credit load at the weekend college was beginning to take its toll. She felt tired constantly. Crabby. Tense.

Well, that's Wren's fault, she decided, crawling into bed. Her muscles groaned their relief as she settled between the soft sheets. *If he'd stop trying to sabotage the court order, I'd have less on my mind.*

13

Nancie wondered if that's really what he was trying to do—get custody of the girls. Wren had always been mild-mannered, easygoing, and sincere—part of the reason she'd married him. And divorced him. After twelve years she'd grown bored living with a spineless amoeba. The man lacked drive and aspiration when it came to bettering himself in the business world, although he was certainly the epitome of a mail carrier: neither rain, nor snow, nor sleet, nor hail. . . .

However, Nancie had wanted—expected—more from her husband than mere faithfulness to a job. She'd envisioned his climbing the ladder of success, but he'd never been interested in advancement.

And then he'd found religion. It happened right after she'd given birth to their youngest. Nancie had had a troublesome pregnancy, and both she and Laura developed some problems after the delivery. Wren's fear for his wife and child had led him to what he termed "the saving knowledge of Christ," and he wasn't the same man afterward. He began taking the Bible literally and attempted to obey its every word.

When Nancie grew concerned about the change in Wren, she talked to her friends at the department store where she'd been working part-time, and they helped her see the real light. Her husband was adopting a philosophy right out of the dark ages, and he'd soon demand that she become some subservient creature. And to think Wren once had had the audacity to tell her the Bible said women should be "keepers at home" and "obedient to their own husbands." When Nancie heard that, it was all over. She had a right to her own life, for pity's sake! As for her children, she loved them with a mother's fierce, protective love, but she knew she could manage her career, college, and raising them, too. Wren knew it as well.

So would he really try to get the girls?

Nancie had to admit she didn't know her ex-husband anymore. Maybe he would. . .except the Wren Nickelson she'd been married to wouldn't have put up a fuss. He would have passively accepted his fate, claiming he was "trusting God." For nearly five years she'd lived with his "trusting God." But she had still hoped he'd take charge of his life and become more assertive. Instead, Wren preferred studying his Bible to reading the self-help books on success that she'd purchased for him. What a disappointment. What a simple man!

Would he really fight me for custody?

Part of Nancie didn't want to believe Wren was capable of such a thing, but the other part didn't trust him. Frankly, she didn't trust men in general. She'd had a few dates since her divorce and had discovered men were all the same. They wanted women to act like deferential ninnies to bolster their macho egos.

Well, not her. Not Nancie Cunningham Nickelson!

❧

"Why can't I live with you?" Alexa asked.

"You do live with me," Wren replied diplomatically. "You live with me on the weekends."

"No, I mean all the time. Why can't I?"

Wren thoughtfully regarded his oldest daughter. Her small face was framed by long, light brown hair. Her cocoa-colored eyes beseeched him with the question she'd asked. "Why?"

"I take it you and your mother aren't getting along any better than last week."

"She hates me," Alexa said, pouting from across the dining-room table. Wren's typewriter and a small pile of his work-in-progress occupied one end, while he and his daughters breakfasted at the other.

"Your mother does not hate you," Wren assured her. "Why do you think that?" He forked in a bite of pancakes and chewed, waiting for the reply.

"I look like you, Dad," the eleven year old stated precociously, "and Mom hates you." A little sob threatened to strangle her. "Now she hates me, too."

"Nonsense, Alexa." Wren set down his fork, stood, and walked around the table. Hunkering beside his daughter, he gathered her slim form onto his knee. She wrapped her arms around his neck. "Your mother loves you very much." He swallowed hard. While he knew he spoke the truth, it hurt to think Nancie hated him. What had he ever done to her? A hot, white-lightning anger, mingled with profound pain, caused his chest muscles to constrict. And for that moment, he hated her right back.

No. . .no, I don't, he thought, his reason slowly returning. He didn't hate his ex-wife. He despised the fact that she'd severed their marriage, and he abhorred his oldest daughter's anguish—an obvious result of their divorce. But no matter what Nancie did or would ever do, Wren knew in his heart he could never hate her. Not only did he realize that that would equate to murder in God's eyes, but very simply, he had loved Nancie far too long and far too deeply.

He still did, although it wasn't always easy.

And that's why he continued to feel wounded—even after a year and a half.

"Dad, she's so mean," Alexa sobbed into his shoulder. "She yells at me all the time. Please, can't I live with you?"

Wren took a deep breath and had to wonder if hormones were at work in his oldest daughter. *Already?* He grimaced.

"Dad, please?"

"Shh, honey—you're wrong. Your mother loves you. But I'll speak with her. Maybe we can work something out." Wren glanced across the table at Laura, who happily ate her pancakes, seemingly unaffected by her older sister's outburst.

Alexa quieted and lifted her chin off of Wren's shoulder. "Do you promise to talk to Mom?"

"I promise."

The girl appeared somewhat mollified.

"Are we still going to the picnic, Daddy?" Laura asked, wiping her syrup-covered mouth on the sleeve of her pink nightie.

Setting Alexa back on her chair, Wren stood and smiled at the seven year old. "We sure are, so hurry up and finish your breakfast. Both of you."

Picking up his plate, he walked into the small kitchen of the lower flat he rented, silently dreading a confrontation with Nancie. She knew how to chew him up, spit him out, and make him feel about two feet high.

George wouldn't be afraid of his ex-wife, Wren mused as the image of his main character flitted across his mind. *George would stand up to her.* He grinned. *Better yet, George would grab hold of Nan, pull her into his arms, and kiss her until she came to her senses.* Wren paused, frowning. *Or would he kiss her senseless. . . ?*

"Daddy, I'm all done," Laura announced, bringing in her plate from the dining room.

Wren snapped to attention and reached for the syrupy stoneware. "Thanks, baby."

She smiled up at him adoringly. "Now I'm gonna get dressed."

"Good girl."

Alexa was next to bring in her plate. "I'll wash the dishes for you," she offered.

"Great. I'll dry."

They made a good team, and soon the task was nearly completed. Peering at his daughter as he dried the last of the utensils, Wren had to admit that Alexa did resemble his side of the family, while Laura looked more like her mother. But he highly doubted Nancie would ever hold her physical appearance against their oldest daughter.

Or would she?

Well, he thought wearily, *I'm going to have to talk to her and find out.*

⁂

"Mrs. Fagan. . .about my grade. . .a D? How could you have given me a D on my speech?"

The instructor, a petite brunette, gave Nancie a tight smile. "I didn't think you conveyed the true purpose behind the women's rights movement. Mary Wollstonecraft advocated educating women so they would be better wives, not so they would shun their station in life. You said some women were slaves in their homes, but housework has nothing to do with women's rights and education. Housework is a part of life in general." The instructor lifted a brow. "I have to do housework, and I have a master's degree."

Nancie glanced around the classroom, relieved to see that most of the other students had gone and that those remaining were out of earshot. "I was referring to housewife mentality as opposed to a woman wanting a career outside the home."

The instructor shrugged. "I felt it was a weak argument and certainly not the cornerstone for women's rights. I know a lot of bright, well-educated women who run their households better than some business professionals manage their offices."

"But—"

"I'm sorry, Nancie. Your speech sounded more like it was based on bitterness than fact."

"Bitterness? I beg your pardon?"

"Look, I've got to go. You're welcome to discuss this further with the dean of our department and appeal the grade. However, I don't think your speech warranted anything more than a D."

The woman turned on her heel. Nancie stood open-mouthed, gaping after the instructor who was leaving the classroom. All her hard work. All her research. Her speech had been worth much more than a D—the information she'd provided was worth at least a B!

Feeling someone tap her on the shoulder, Nancie spun around and peered into the face of a middle-aged, heavyset woman with blond, frizzy hair.

"We call her Fagan the Dragon."

Nancie lifted a questioning brow. "What?"

"Our instructor. Her name is Louise Fagan. This is the second time I've had her for a teacher, and I can attest to the fact that she's earned the nickname Fagan the Dragon."

"Oh. . ." Nancie didn't feel like discussing the matter with another student and began shoving her text and notebook into her red canvas shoulder bag.

"So you're divorced, too, huh?"

Nancie gave the woman an annoyed glance. "How'd you know?"

"Takes one to know one, I guess. My husband left me for another woman ten years ago. I carried a lot of anger inside me for a long time. Who wouldn't?"

"For your information," Nancie replied curtly, "my husband did not leave me. I left him. And I am not angry or bitter, contrary to Mrs. Fagan's theory. . .and yours, too, obviously." Throwing her bag over her shoulder, she added, "And I'll thank you to mind your own business from now on."

"I'm just trying to help."

Nancie didn't reply, but marched out of the classroom.

"Deny it all you want," her classmate called after her, "but you're going to have to face your feelings sometime."

Oh, what does she know? Nancie thought with a huff as she left the building for the parking lot, striding purposely toward her car. *I don't have a resentful bone in my body. I'm just confident and successful and they're jealous.* Reaching her white sports car, she opened the door and threw her book bag into the passenger seat with more force than necessary before she slid behind the wheel. *I don't need them. . . . I don't need anyone. I'm going all the way to the top and no one is going to stop me!*

three

Risa Vitalis saw him walk into the picnic area of the park with two girls and excused herself from the conversation she'd been having with one of her coworkers. She'd been hoping he would show up today at the annual postal workers' picnic.

"Wren!" she called, smiling and waving. She immediately took note of his light blue polo shirt and well-worn jeans. He looked good—real good. "I saved us a spot over here," she added, pointing to a table in the shade that she'd covered with a brightly-patterned plastic cloth.

Nodding, he strode toward her, while the girls took off in the opposite direction, heading for swings and jungle-gym apparatus. As he neared, Risa's smile grew.

"I'm glad you decided to come, Wren."

He shrugged his broad shoulders and easily swung the cooler onto the table. "I wanted to take the girls somewhere today, and seeing as the weather's so nice—"

"You mean you didn't come because you knew I'd be here?" she asked, with an exaggerated pout.

Wren gave her a sideways glance, but his tiny smile indicated the embarrassment he felt.

"Aw, I'm just kidding. But you knew that, right?"

"Yeah, I knew it."

And Risa knew it, too. . . . That is, she knew Wren Nickelson didn't share her romantic interest. He didn't ask her out on dates or lead her to believe he ever would. He'd made it clear—they were just friends. But that didn't stop Risa from dreaming about him at night—or trying to win his heart by day.

"Want a pop? I brought some."

Wren shook his dark brown head. "No, thanks."

He sat down on the bench, leaning his elbows on the table-top. He gazed off in the direction of where his daughters were at play while Risa made good use of the moment and admired the man. His face was clean-shaven and already tanned from walking his route. His arms looked strong—from lifting and carrying heavy mailbags, she supposed—and Risa wished she'd one day feel them around her. . . .

Now if only he'd take off that silly wedding band, she thought as the gold ring on his left hand glinted in the sunshine.

As if he sensed the weight of her stare, Wren turned and looked at her.

She blinked. "So those are your daughters, huh?" she asked lamely in an effort to cover her enamored scrutiny. Clearing her throat, she sat down beside him.

"Yep." He fairly beamed. "See the one in the pink T-shirt? That's Alexa, my oldest. The little blond one in the yellow bibs is Laura."

"They're adorable—even at this distance. I can't wait to meet them." Risa scooted closer to him, then crossed her legs. "Have you done your description assignment for Monday night's class?"

Wren looked her way and his dark brown eyes twinkled. "Not yet. You?"

"All done. Want to read it?"

"Sure. You brought it along?"

"Uh-huh." She stood, found her vinyl tote, and pulled out the green folder. She plucked the neatly typed page of description from one of the pockets and handed it to Wren.

While he read, she reclaimed her seat and nibbled her lower lip nervously.

Finally, he looked over at her and smiled. "It's very good."

"Really? You wouldn't just say that, would you?"

"No."

Risa nodded. She believed him. Wren was honest to a fault.

"But I hope you don't mind my saying it is rather dark." He handed the paper back to her. "It reads like something out of a Stephen King novel."

"I was describing my stepfather. He's always reminded me of a reptile: beady eyes set too far apart on his wide face, thin lips. . . ."

"Yeah, I get the picture." Wren tipped his head quizzically. "Doesn't sound like you're very fond of him."

"I'm not. He was abusive."

"Oh, Risa. . .I'm sorry." Wren's tone was warm and sympathetic.

Somewhat embarrassed, she dropped her gaze to the page she held between her hands. Then she peeked up at him. "I'll bet you're a wonderful father to your two girls, aren't you?"

"I sure try," he said with a small lift of his shoulders and a weary-sounding sigh. "I wish I could be more a part of their lives."

"Divorce is tough. I was about twelve when my folks divorced. My mom remarried the next year and I hated my stepfather. Still do. I was his verbal punching bag."

Wren stretched a comforting arm around her shoulders, giving her a little hug, and Risa had to resist the urge to snuggle against him.

"Finally my mother felt sorry for me and sent me to live with my natural father. I went through a lot of counseling. For a long time I couldn't trust anyone. I didn't feel safe enough." She paused, hoping he would somehow understand the depth of the words about to pass through her lips. "But I feel very safe with you."

He didn't disappoint her. "Risa, I'm. . .I'm flattered you feel that way."

She smiled. "It's true."

Wren brought his arm back to his side, much to her disappointment. "Well, I've got to give the glory to the Lord for that one," he said, gazing out across the expanse of plush green lawn.

"What do you mean?" she asked with a puzzled frown.

"You feel safe with me because I'm a Christian."

"No. I've met men who were religious and I wasn't comfortable in their presence at all."

"Risa, just because a guy acts religious doesn't mean he's a Christian. Being born again isn't about religion. It's about God's grace."

She replied with a shrug. In truth, she didn't want to talk about God. She was a little afraid of Him. She figured if she didn't bother God, He wouldn't bother her. "Well, anyway," she said, changing the subject back to her past, "the counseling helped, and I'm okay with everything now."

"Except you still hate your stepdad."

"Always will."

"Then you aren't really okay, Risa. You need to forgive him."

"Are you nuts?" She stood and put her assignment back in her folder. "What my stepfather did to me is unforgivable."

Wren didn't answer.

"I hope you noticed how calm I sound."

"Uh-huh."

"Well, that just proves I'm okay. I can talk about my stepdad, I can even write about him, and I don't feel angry or depressed anymore."

"That's a mark of healing, no doubt about it."

"But?" Risa sensed more was coming.

"But forgiveness is the ultimate test."

She shook her head before combing several fingers through her unruly, rust-colored curls. "I can't forgive him."

"No, you can't," Wren stated emphatically. "Not in your own strength you can't. But with God's help, you can." He suddenly chuckled. "Didn't think you'd hear a sermon on a Saturday, did you?"

With a little laugh, she sat back down next to him. "I'll

take it from you, Wren, because I know you're not a hypocrite. I know you mean what you say." She grinned coquettishly. "Except I'd like to change your mind about a few things you've told me."

"Like what?"

His boyish innocence caused Risa to laugh. "I'm flirting with you," she stated emphatically.

Wren's eyes lit up with understanding. "I'm glad you pointed that out," he said as an embarrassed expression crossed his face. "Guess I'm a dunce."

"No, you're delightful."

He met her gaze for several long moments, causing the hope in her heart to soar unfettered.

"I think I'd better go check on my girls."

He stood and, before Risa could reply, three of their coworkers appeared, asking to share the picnic table. Much to her dismay, Wren gave them an enthusiastic welcome.

❧

Nancie barely made it through her classes Sunday morning—it was a good thing they only lasted until noon. As she drove away from the college, she felt the tension melt from her muscles. She was exhausted, so exhausted she could hardly think straight. But her final exams were now over. She'd completed another year of school.

As she maneuvered her car through the streets of Milwaukee, she thought about calling a few friends and celebrating this feat—two years of college, finished. But mulling over several names, she realized that she'd lost touch with many of her old acquaintances in the past eighteen months. Besides, some of them were Wren's friends now, not hers. Divorce had an ugly way of causing people to choose sides.

This is dumb, Nancie thought. *I have lots of friends. Why can't I think of a single soul to call?*

If her mother were alive, Nancie knew she'd call her. Mom would have been thrilled. She'd always said, "Women can have it all, but we settle for so much less." And Nancie supposed twenty-seven years of marriage to a factory worker and veritable "couch potato" had taught her mother that. As much as Nancie loved her father, she considered him something of a disappointment.

Like Wren.

"Well, I'm not settling, Mom," she uttered out loud in prayerlike fashion. "You'd be proud of me. I have a good job, beautiful kids, a comfortable apartment with new furniture. I'm bettering myself by earning a college degree. . . ."

Nancie frowned. *So why can't I think of some friends to call?*

Cruising along the lakefront and then down Lake Drive, she came to a halt at the stoplight on Capitol Drive in Shorewood. The village was one square mile in diameter and bordered Lake Michigan. Nancie hadn't enjoyed living in Shorewood. She'd wanted to live in Whitefish Bay, the neighboring suburb with more class. However, Wren had refused, saying they couldn't afford it. He never even tried. But after she dumped the guy, Nancie had gotten what she wanted—a Whitefish Bay address.

When they divorced, she was awarded the house in Shorewood, but promptly sold it and made quite a bit of money. Nancie bought the girls and herself some needed things—new clothes, shoes, bikes—and then socked the rest away in the bank for her college education. Of course, Nancie had a bit of savings left from which she occasionally drew in those times when her paychecks didn't quite cover all the bills, her car payment, installment on the new furniture, and the rent. But, thankfully, Wren paid child support. That helped.

She gasped in sudden understanding. *That's it! That's why he wants custody. He thinks he's going to save money.* Indignation swelled within her. *Well, he's got another think coming!*

Nancie turned off Lake Drive and headed for Wren's place, deciding she'd pick up the girls early and take them some-place special for dinner tonight—after she gave that ex-husband of hers a piece of her mind.

Whatever's left of it to give, she silently quipped. Moments later, she pulled up alongside the curb in front of his duplex.

She gazed at the house before exiting the car. It looked somewhat shabby even for a Shorewood residence. The yellow wooden siding had faded, chipped, and peeled. The brown trim was in need of paint as well, and the rickety front porch required attention—soon.

Why doesn't he find a better place to live? she wondered, making her way up the walk. She recalled Wren saying an investment company owned the building, and obviously it wasn't concerned with the property's upkeep. The neighbors must be furious.

She rang the doorbell. No answer. She waited. Nothing. Then, as she headed for her car, she heard giggles coming from the backyard. Soon Alexa and Laura came strolling around the side of the house, dressed in their Sunday best. Wren was behind them, wearing tan trousers and a navy jacket with coordinating tie.

Church. Of course. Nancie had forgotten.

"Mom. What are you doing here?"

She tried to ignore Alexa's frown, although it angered her. Wasn't her oldest child glad to see her?

"Hi, Mumma," Laura said, looking a bit confused. "It's not time for you to come yet."

Seeing her, Wren halted in his tracks. His expression was a mixture of their daughters', sort of an uncertain grimace. "Hi, Nancie. Did I miss something? Had you planned to pick up the girls early today?"

"Well, yes. . .except this is rather spur of the moment. I guess I should have phoned."

"I'm not going!" Alexa said crossly as she folded her arms

over the red, white, and blue plaid jumper she wore.

"Nancie, I think you and I had better talk."

"Yes, I think you're right," she said through a clenched jaw.

Alexa turned to Wren. "Tell her I don't want to live with her anymore. She's mean!"

Nancie's eyes widened in shock. "Alexa!"

"Tell her, Dad."

Wren gave the child a stern look. "I won't have you talking about your mother like that. What does the fifth commandment say?"

Alexa tucked her chin and grudgingly answered, "Honor thy father and thy mother."

"Did you just honor your mother?"

She shrugged.

"Lex?"

"No," she ground out at last. "But it's true."

Wren lowered his voice. "And didn't I tell you I would take care of the situation?"

"Yes, but. . ."

Alexa clamped her mouth shut as Wren narrowed his gaze in silent warning. Nancie had to admit to being somewhat impressed by the way he'd handled their cantankerous eleven-year-old. Inevitably, Nancie ended up losing her patience and raising her voice.

Pulling his keys from his pants pocket, he handed them to Alexa. "Take your little sister inside and make us some lunch, okay?"

" 'Kay." She took the keys. "C'mon, Laura."

The girl followed, but paused on the top step of the porch. "Daddy?" She glanced briefly at Nancie before looking back at Wren. "Can we still go to the birthday party this afternoon?"

"We'll see, baby. Oh, and here," he said, shrugging out of his jacket. "Take this into the house for me."

She nodded agreeably and entered the house.

Wren turned and faced Nancie.

She took a deep breath and prepared for battle.

"I understand that you and Alexa aren't getting along," he began.

"We'd get along just fine if you'd stop poisoning my relationship with her."

"Me?"

"Don't look so surprised. I know you're talking behind my back. You're hoping the girls end up hating me so you can take custody."

"That's ridiculous. I've never said a bad word about you to our children. To anyone!"

"You expect me to believe that?"

Wren thought it over a moment. "Yes!"

Nancie tapered her gaze, wondering if he told the truth. "Have I ever lied to you?"

"I've never caught you at it, no."

Wren rolled his eyes and put his hands on his hips. "What about the custody issue?"

"What about it?" he asked.

"Are you planning to take me back to court?"

"No. We're adults. We should be able to settle this without dragging it into court."

Nancie folded her arms, lifting a stubborn chin. "What do you suggest?"

Looking across the yard, Wren squinted into the sunshine. "I think Alexa should live with me for a couple of weeks. Maybe that'll alleviate some of the tension between you two."

"And where do you think this 'tension' is coming from?"

He brought his gaze back and considered her for a good measure of time. "Nancie, that's something you're going to have to figure out. I don't know what's going on with you. I only know what Alexa's told me."

"What's that?"

"That you yell at her. . .you're mean. . .that you hate her."

"Oh, give me a break, Wren. That's crazy. I don't hate my own daughter."

"Alexa told me yesterday morning that you hate me, and because she resembles me, you hate her, too."

Nancie shook her head, dismayed. "I don't hate you, Wren. I hated being married to you."

A look of hurt flashed across his face, but Nancie ignored it. Wren needed to hear the truth. . .again. Perhaps he'd finally get it through his thick head and take off his wedding ring. It irked her that he still wore it. She'd sold hers.

Taking a step forward, Nancie glared into his brown eyes. "Marriage to you, Wren, was the greatest oppression I've ever experienced."

He didn't even wince. . .this time. "Well, you got what you wanted. You're free to do whatever you like with your life."

"And I'm doing it."

"So why aren't you happy?"

"I am happy," Nancie retorted. "I'm very happy!"

"You don't act like it. You don't sound like it. When I see you coming, I cringe, wondering if you're going to pick another fight with me. You're a bully. Don't you think the girls pick up on that stuff? Alexa especially, being the oldest. You can't fool them, Nancie. Our daughters see a very angry woman when they look at you."

She cursed, and this time Wren did wince. "For your information, I've been under a lot of stress. I work full-time and attend weekend college, and I have to manage my home and kids."

"Don't complain to me about that." He narrowed his gaze furiously. "And don't you dare take it out on my children."

Nancie suddenly felt like she was losing ground. Wren had never argued with her before. He always gave in to her demands. Why was he suddenly standing up for himself?

Because he's not fighting for himself, she soon realized. *He's fighting for his daughters.*

Inhaling deeply, Nancie decided on a different tactic. "You know, Wren," she began carefully and in a softer tone of voice, "the girls have it so good with you. You see them on the weekends, you play with them and show them a good time. I get them during the week and have to be the disciplinarian. I have to tell them to turn off the television and do their homework. I insist they help with the dishes, straighten up the apartment, and make their beds every morning. That's why Alexa thinks I'm 'mean.' Of course she'd much rather live with you."

"Then let's allow her to stay with me for a while and she can see what it's really like."

Nancie arched a brow. "And if I refuse?"

"Then you'll probably have to take Alexa kicking and screaming, because she's made up her mind that she's not going home with you."

She'd lost. Nancie knew it. She could take on Wren single-handedly, but she couldn't fight Alexa, too. However, her innermost fear was that Laura would follow suit.

"You know what, Wren?" Nancie said with a clenched jaw, "I think I do hate you."

He kind of shrugged. "I don't doubt it."

She turned on her heel. "I'll be back to pick up Laura at eight o'clock," she shot over her shoulder.

Without a reply Wren turned, walked up to the front door, and entered the house.

four

Wren finished writing the next scene of his novel, then sat back in the dining-room chair. He liked this next sequence of events: George and Nan just had a spat, and George emerged the victor. But George always did. Nan had nothing on him.

Recalling the confrontation with Nancie this afternoon, Wren was quite surprised by his own relentlessness. He'd stood his ground for probably the first time in years. Well, Nancie already hated him. What did he have to lose?

Lord, he silently prayed, *it's getting harder and harder to love that woman.* And yet Wren knew he did. There would always be a place in his heart for Nancie. . .although Risa had somehow found a place there, too. He enjoyed her company. She was a good friend.

Looking back at his typewritten page, Wren suddenly wondered if he ought to kill off Nan and twist the plot so that George could marry Lucia, the redheaded Italian beauty who was crazy in love with him. He grinned. The scenario had definite possibilities.

Hearing a soft utterance, he glanced over his shoulder at Laura, who had fallen asleep on the couch. He looked at his wristwatch. Ten-thirty. Where in the world was Nancie? She should have arrived two hours ago.

Scooting the chair backward, he stood and walked into the kitchen, peeking into the girls' bedroom on the way in. He found Alexa in bed, sleeping peacefully. After grabbing a cold soda from the fridge, Wren strolled back to the dining room, where he intended to resume his writing.

Until the phone rang.

"Wren? This is Nancie."

"Where are you?" he asked impatiently. "I thought you were coming at eight."

"I know. I'm. . .well, I'm at the hospital," she said. Her voice sounded strained. "I got mugged tonight."

At once, Wren's agitation became concern. "Are you all right?"

"Yeah. . .except I needed a couple of stitches. Everything happened so fast that I don't even remember what I hit my head on. Whatever it was, it gave me a nice gash above my ear."

"Oh, Nancie, I'm sorry," Wren replied sincerely.

"What's worse is that the jerk got my purse containing all my money, my keys, and my credit cards."

"Did you get a good look at the person who jumped you?"

"Not really. But I heard his voice, so I know it was a man."

Wren paused. "It could have been worse, Nancie. I'm glad all you got was a laceration."

"I know." She cleared her throat. "When I think how easily I could have been beaten or murdered. . .or raped."

A brief interval of silence lapsed between them before Nancie spoke again.

"Umm. . .Wren?" she asked carefully. "I wondered if you could pick me up and drive me home. The manager of my apartment complex said she'd let me in once I get there."

He hesitated before answering. On the one hand, he wanted to do Nancie this favor. On the other, he was still stinging from the hateful words she'd hurled at him this afternoon.

"The girls are sleeping. Couldn't you take a cab and pay the driver when you get to your apartment?"

She expelled an audible sigh. "All the money I had was in my wallet. My checkbook was in there, too. I don't have any cash at home, so I'll have to go to the bank tomorrow in order to make a withdrawal. I didn't even have change to phone you. The hospital is letting me make a couple of calls from the registration desk."

"Yeah, okay. . ." Wren didn't see any other options. "I'll be there soon."

"Thanks," she murmured before hanging up.

Clicking off the portable phone, Wren looked over at Laura's sleeping form. Then he threw a glance toward the girls' bedroom, in which Alexa slept. He hated to disturb them. They needed their rest. They had school tomorrow.

Just then a loud thunk above the ceiling caught his attention. Staring upward, he guessed one of his three neighbors had dropped something. He supposed he could ask Julie to stay with the girls. She was probably still awake and studying for finals.

Walking through the kitchen, he opened the back door and quietly climbed the back stairs. Two young women and a rather strange-looking young man lived up here. All were students of the university, but of the three, Julie seemed the most responsible. Wren felt confident she would watch the girls tonight, she'd done it before, and Alexa and Laura liked her.

Arriving at the door, he knocked.

❧

The cool night breeze caused Nancie to shiver as she stood outside the emergency room entrance waiting for Wren. But at least the throbbing in her head had dissipated, thanks to the doctor who'd given her a dose of pain medication. She hugged herself tightly, trying to keep warm, and decided that this had been the most frightening night of her life. She'd felt perfectly safe, walking to her car at 7:30 in broad daylight. And she'd been confident in her ability to take care of herself, having taken a self-defense course last year. How had that man overpowered her so effortlessly? How had he sneaked up behind her so quickly? Suddenly Nancie wasn't so sure of anything anymore. Even now, standing here under the lighted entryway of the hospital, she felt alone and afraid.

Just then she spotted Wren's car and sighed audibly in relief. She watched as he drove into the circular drive and pulled up in front of her.

"Thanks for picking me up," Nancie said, opening the passenger door and climbing in.

When Wren didn't reply, she gave him a sideways glance.

"You sure you're okay?" he finally asked.

Nancie conceded a little nod. At this point she wasn't sure if she was "okay" or not. Something had happened tonight—something that had caused her self-confidence to splinter like rotten wood.

"What happened?" Wren asked. "I mean, I know what happened, but how did it happen?"

"I was at a nightclub downtown. . .celebrating."

"By yourself?"

Nancie clenched her jaw at Wren's perceptiveness. "What makes you think I was alone?" she ground out.

"Well, for starters, you wouldn't have phoned me if you'd been with friends. I'm the guy you said you hated this afternoon, remember?"

She didn't answer. She couldn't. What he said was true. Once more that sinking, isolated feeling enveloped her.

"You want the truth, Wren? Okay, I'll tell you the truth." Her voice sounded hard to her own ears because of the hurt she felt inside. "Yes. I was alone. I've completed two years of college now and I wanted to celebrate, but I couldn't think of anyone to invite. I wanted to take the girls to dinner. . . . That's why I came over this afternoon."

"Why didn't you just say so, Nancie? We would have rejoiced with you."

"No, you wouldn't have. We hate each other." She folded her arms in front of her and stared out the window. There wasn't much traffic this late on a Sunday night. Even the nightclub had been sparsely populated.

"I don't hate you. Never have," Wren said softly after an interminable pause.

Nancie swung her gaze around and gave him a perplexing

stare. "You should hate me, Wren. But that's your problem. You don't think like normal people."

"Is that why you phoned me tonight?" he asked, somewhat sarcastically. "Because, not being 'normal,' you knew I'd pick you up? I presume a normal person would have let you fend for yourself after what happened this afternoon."

Nancie closed her eyes briefly, swallowing her indignation. "Okay, Wren, I suppose I deserved that. You're right. I called you because I knew you'd come. And. . .well, thanks."

Silence filled the car for the rest of the drive to her apartment. Climbing out of the car, Nancie noticed the bright moon, clear sky, and sharp stars. Then she noticed something else; the lampposts surrounding the parking lot were off. An eerie premonition gripped her heart. Suppose the thief was in her apartment, waiting for her? He had her address, her keys. . . .

"Um. . .Wren?"

He was already out of the car, obviously planning to see her inside. She wasn't going to have to ask.

When they reached the small lobby, Nancie located the manager of the complex and obtained the spare key to her place. Wren dutifully walked up the steps behind her and followed her to her door. Frightened silly over the thought of her attacker possibly being in her home, Nancie's hand trembled as she tried to insert the key into the lock.

"Must be the pain medication the doctor gave me," she muttered to Wren. She hoped it covered her ineptitude, which embarrassed her terribly.

Wren took the key from her fingers and unlocked the door. He stepped inside first and, having been there numerous times, flipped the wall switch, causing the matching lamps on each end table to flood the living room with light.

No one had been lurking in the shadows, and relief filled Nancie's being.

Next, Wren walked into the small kitchen and turned on the light. He repeated the procedure in the hallway, the girls' bedroom, and Nancie's room before reentering the living-room area.

"I think you'll be okay. I even checked the closets and under beds."

Chagrin washed over her, from her hairline down. She had to smile. "How'd you know, Wren? How'd you know I was scared out of my wits, thinking someone might be hiding in here?"

This time Wren looked embarrassed. "We were married for twelve years, Nancie. That's how I knew."

"But I'm different now," she argued. "How could you possibly have guessed I felt so frightened tonight?"

He shrugged. "I suppose some things never change."

Nancie glanced at the beige carpeting beneath her feet. "Perhaps not."

Then Wren surprised her further by stepping forward, placing his hands on her shoulders, and giving her a sound kiss on the cheek. Smiling into her eyes, he told her good night.

As she watched him exit her apartment, Nancie experienced a myriad of emotions. Anger because Wren obviously still cared for her when she didn't want him to. Relief that he did still care and was willing to be there when she needed him. Remorse over the way their marriage had ended. And most of all, disappointment—because Nancie realized tonight that she was not the brave, self-reliant woman she'd led herself to believe.

five

Nancie made the appropriate phone calls to her credit card lenders and the bank the next morning to report her wallet stolen. Shortly before noon, a locksmith completed the task of changing the locks in her apartment and the door in the lobby. Then, spare car key in hand, she took a taxi downtown and retrieved her vehicle. By 1:30, she arrived at work.

Setting her new purse on her desk, she checked in with her boss before heading to the cafeteria, where she intended to purchase a can of cold soda. But as she neared the entryway, the sound of male voices caused her to pause there in the hall.

"Don't bother asking Nancie Nickelson," one of the men said. "She won't be interested. She never donates to our pizza lunches."

"Why not?" asked someone else.

"Because she thinks she's too good to eat with the rest of us," said the first man, and Nancie soon recognized his voice—it belonged to Bob Mitchell, a coworker.

"She doesn't have a friend in this entire company," said another man whom Nancie guessed to be Craig Harris. He and Bob were thick as thieves.

"So, she's one of those hoity-toity females, eh?"

"No, Nancie's more like a blond broomstick rider," came the reply before a whoop of laughter broke out.

Outside the door, Nancie fumed. How dare those imbeciles talk about her like that! She turned, preparing to enter the cafeteria and verbally blast them into orbit, but then she thought up a different plan of action. What if she killed them with kindness and made Bob and Craig look like the idiots they really were?

She grinned and decided to do it. Taking a deep breath, she walked through the doorway.

"Hi, guys," she said pleasantly, throwing them a quick glance.

Their laughter subsided.

"Oh, hi, Nancie," Bob said. "Come over here and meet Pete Larsen, our newest employee."

After purchasing a soft drink, Nancie sauntered over to the large, round table at which the three men sat. "Hello, Pete; nice to meet you," she said in a friendly voice. Sticking out her hand, she gave his a firm welcoming shake. "I'm sure you'll enjoy working for this company. It's one of the best in the nation."

"Thanks," he replied, looking a bit uneasy. "I'm sure I will."

"So, Nancie," Craig said, sitting back in his chair and wearing a confident smirk, "wanna go in on our next pizza luncheon? It's scheduled for Wednesday."

She manufactured a velveteen smile. "Sure. That'd be great. Sign me up." Glancing briefly at all of them, she added, "See you guys later."

Dead silence followed in her wake and Nancie almost laughed out loud. What a bunch of losers.

With her head held high, she walked back to her desk; however, by the time she reached it, she had begun mulling over what she'd heard. "She thinks she's too good to eat with the rest of us. . .she doesn't have a friend in this entire company. . .a blond broomstick rider."

Nancie flipped the switch on her computer and wondered if what they'd said of her was true. Of course it wasn't. . . except she couldn't think of a solitary comrade here at work. She had her acquaintances, of course, but no one with whom she shared confidences.

Okay, so that part is true, she thought, feeling somewhat defensive. *But it's only because I've been so busy. With a routine like mine, who could find the time to make friends!*

She reached for a stack of papers on her desk and for no apparent reason Alexa came to mind. Nancie's heart ached as she remembered how her oldest daughter had called her "mean." Did Alexa really think her own mother hated her?

Sorrow filled Nancie's heart. She loved Alexa deeply. Sure, they'd had their scrapes, but they were a result of Nancie's attempts to correct her daughter's bad behavior, not to mention her lousy attitude.

Blond broomstick rider. The cutting depiction of her character rang in Nancie's memory. Is that really how coworkers saw her? Is that how her own daughter viewed her? A wicked witch of some sort? Next she recalled how Wren had called her a "bully."

Uneasiness crept over her, but she did her best to ignore it, and she forced herself to concentrate on her work for the rest of the afternoon.

❧

Wren finished up his mail route and then picked up the girls at Ruth's house.

"You're early," Ruth stated with a note of surprise when she opened the front door. "The girls don't usually get picked up until about five-thirty."

"Yeah, I know. . . . I hope this doesn't pose any problems for you, but Nancie and I talked yesterday and decided Alexa would live with me for a while until the tension ebbs between the two of them. I figured as long as I'm picking up Alexa, I might as well get Laura, too. Nancie can pick up Laura at my place after work."

"That's fine. I could smell a change in the wind when you dropped the girls off this morning." She tipped her head as a curious expression crossed her face. "Did Nancie really agree to those terms?"

"For now." He couldn't help but chuckle at Ruth's incredulous, wide-eyed stare. In fact, he felt much the same way— awestruck—and the small victory had boosted his confidence by leaps and bounds.

That's how George would have handled things, he mused in the front hallway as Ruth rounded up his daughters. However, Wren knew in his heart that any battles won with Nancie stemmed purely from God's grace. Yesterday afternoon's triumph was, very simply, a blessing from heaven.

Shifting his stance, Wren leaned on the doorjamb. *I've got to make sure that George gives the glory to the Lord for his successes,* he decided, thinking over his story line. He was ready to begin writing chapter three, and his fingers itched to get to the typewriter keys.

"Da-ad," Alexa said, bringing Wren out of his faraway thoughts, "me and Laura are ready to go."

He smiled, feeling a tad embarrassed. "Great."

Together the three of them walked to the car. The sky was overcast, the air cool. Climbing in behind the wheel, Wren wondered what to do with Alexa tonight while he was at writing class. He supposed he could ask Julie, his neighbor upstairs, but he hated to bother her again.

He drove the half-mile from Whitefish Bay to Shorewood and parked in front of his house. The girls jumped out of the car, grabbing their backpacks and spring jackets, and dashed to the porch. Wren met them there moments later and unlocked the door.

"What's for supper, Daddy?" Laura said, plopping down on the sofa. "I'm hungry."

"To tell you the truth, I hadn't thought about it." Wren began unbuttoning his shirt as he headed for the shower. "Stick in one of those videos we got from the library Saturday, and I'll think about making you two something to eat while I'm washing up and changing."

Entering his bedroom, he heard muttered replies. Then, as he removed his uniform and pulled on a bathrobe, he mentally took stock of his cupboards and refrigerator. He hadn't gone grocery shopping in a long while. There wasn't much in the way of ingredients for a healthy meal, although he had dry cereal, milk, eggs, and a loaf of bread. Maybe he could make them breakfast for dinner.

After a long hot shower, Wren shrugged back into his terry cloth robe and left the steamy bathroom. In his room once more, he dressed in blue jeans and a Wisconsin Badgers sweatshirt before stuffing his stockinged feet into white leather athletic shoes.

As he sat on the bed tying the laces, he suddenly smelled something—something good. Garlic. Tomato. Maybe pizza. His mouth watered.

"Alexa, what are you doing?" he called, leaving his bedroom and strolling to the kitchen. "Are you cooking?" He stopped short at the doorway. His eldest daughter was cooking, all right. Laura, too. But they had some help—Risa. Wren smiled. "What are you doing here?"

"I'm creating a Caesar salad. What does it look like I'm doing?"

He smacked his palm to his forehead. "Silly me. I should have known."

The girls giggled at the exchange, and Risa grinned. "Seriously, though, I made up a pan of lasagna last night," she explained, "and I thought I'd share the leftovers. When I arrived, Alexa and Laura told me they were hungry, so I decided to take liberties in your kitchen." She paused, and her hazel-eyed gaze bore into his. "I hope you don't mind."

"Not at all," Wren replied, looking away and focusing on his daughters. Boy, was he glad he'd picked them up this evening. They'd act as chaperons, of sorts. He enjoyed Risa's company, but he was beginning to enjoy it far too much. Sure, he was divorced, unattached by the world's standards; but he felt certain that dating and marrying any woman other than his ex-wife was not in God's plan for his life. The Lord had made it clear to Wren that he'd taken a vow "till death do we part," and now he had an obligation to uphold that promise. Besides, Risa wasn't a Christian. That was another reason he couldn't entertain thoughts of developing a romantic relationship with her.

"Dinner will be ready shortly," she said, flipping a thick portion of her curly carrot-orange hair over her shoulder.

"Great. Maybe I'll watch the news for a while."

Risa followed him into the living room. "Are you mad at me, Wren, for barging in on you like this?"

He pivoted. "Not at all." He shook his head, chastening himself for giving her that impression. Looking her squarely in the eyes, he added, "But I do think there's a guy out there, somewhere, who's more deserving of your culinary skills than I am."

"Oh, yeah?" She tipped her head sassily. "Find him. I've been searching for years, Wren. You're the most decent man I've met so far." Raising a brow, she smirked. "And you're not bad-looking, either."

A flash of chagrin warmed his face. "You sure know how to get to a guy."

"I'm trying," she replied impishly before spinning around and heading toward the kitchen.

"Risa. . ."

"I know, I know," she said over her shoulder with a backward glance. "We're just friends."

❧

Nancie stood on the porch and rang Wren's doorbell. She pushed up the sleeve of her blouse and peered at her wristwatch. Six-fifteen. She'd gotten out of work forty-five minutes late only to discover that Wren had picked up the girls. Consequently, she'd had to backtrack over here. An extra trip. . .and she felt so tired. What's more, her head was beginning to pound from yesterday's injury and the stress at the office today.

Suddenly the inside door opened and Laura gazed up at her. "Hi, Mumma."

"Hi, sweetie, can I come in?"

The little girl nodded. Nancie pulled on the screen door and entered the house. The aroma of Italian spices assailed her senses at once, causing her stomach to grumble with hunger. Then she spotted Alexa on the couch with her math book open.

"Did you two eat supper already?"

Laura was the one to answer. "Yep. Lex and me helped Risa make it, too."

"Risa. . . ?"

No sooner had Nancie uttered the name when out from the kitchen stepped a lovely redhead. In two sweeping glances, Nancie noted how well the woman's jeans hugged her slim hips and how the fitted green sweater, with its deep V-neck, complemented her full figure.

"Hi," the woman greeted her as she entered the living room. There was a slight edge to her voice. "I'm Risa Vitalis."

"Nancie Nickelson."

"I figured that's who you were. Wren's ex, huh?"

"That's right." Nancie knew her tone sounded flat, wary. Was this Wren's girlfriend or a very shapely baby-sitter? No, it couldn't be his girlfriend, she silently reasoned. Risa didn't appear to be the kind who would fall for a boring mailman. She must be a neighbor. . . .

"This is Risa, Mumma," Laura said.

"Yes, we just met." She looked at her eldest, who still hadn't uttered a word to her. "Hello, Alexa."

"Hi." The girl didn't even glance up from her textbook.

Nancie sighed. Why did everything in her life suddenly seem so hopeless? "Get your stuff together, Laura. Let's get going."

"Okay."

While Laura collected her belongings, Nancie chanced a look at Risa. To her dismay, the woman was eyeing her speculatively.

"Something wrong?" Nancie asked.

"No. I was just thinking." Risa sat down on the arm of the couch and forced a smile.

"Uh-huh. . ." Nancie couldn't have cared less.

At that moment Wren walked in carrying a dish towel, drying his hands with it. "Hi, Nancie."

"Hi."

"How's your head?"

"It hurts," she said curtly.

"Sorry to hear that." Nancie recognized his nervous expression. She saw him glance at Risa. "Have you two met?"

"Just did," the redhead replied with a genuine smile for Wren. And the way she gazed up at him left no doubt in Nancie's mind as to her intentions. She was definitely not the baby-sitter. The only puzzle was that Wren acted unaware of her adoration.

Nancie's curiosity got the best of her. "Are you two dating?"

"I'm dating him," Risa said with a small laugh, "and I'm striving for reciprocation."

"Knock it off, will you?" Wren replied with a chuckle before bringing his gaze back to Nancie. "We're just friends."

"How nice," Nancie muttered, although she didn't believe a word of it. Friends? Yeah, right.

Then she noticed that Alexa was watching Risa closely and wearing a fond expression. A stab of jealousy pierced her heart. It seemed to Nancie that the Italian beauty was destined to replace her in more ways than one.

"Say, Wren, why don't you ask your ex about tonight?"

The question captivated Nancie's attention. "What about tonight?"

"Forget it, Risa."

"Oh, just ask her. The worst she can say is 'no.' "

A dubious expression waved across his features.

"Ask me what?" The question escaped Nancie's lips with an air of indignation.

He shifted his stance and chewed his lower lip for a brief moment before explaining. "Risa and I have a class tonight and I don't have a sitter for Alexa. We could take her along—"

"Yeah!" the eleven-year-old exclaimed with glee.

"But it does run kind of late," Wren finished despite the interruption. "Besides, you'd be bored, Lex."

"You're taking a class?" Nancie hadn't gotten past that bit of information. It seemed too incredible. For years she'd nagged Wren to further his education in one form or another and better himself, but he'd refused. Now he was actually doing that very thing? Nancie wondered if the voluptuous woman in the snug green sweater had had something to do with it.

Again the pang of jealousy.

"I know you're still recovering from last night's ordeal," Wren continued.

"No. That's all right. I'll stay with the girls." She wasn't sure why she had volunteered so quickly, but Nancie sensed that she had to. For the sake of her relationship with Alexa, if for no other reason. Somehow she had to change her image in her daughter's eyes, and it had to top Alexa's opinion of Risa.

"Are you sure, Nancie?" Wren asked, a tiny frown furrowing his brows.

She nodded. "I'm sure."

"Great," Risa said as she stood up. "We should get going, too. Class starts at seven."

"The girls ate already," Wren stated informatively.

"Yes, Laura told me."

"There's plenty of lasagna left, so help yourself."

"Thanks."

Risa found her large black satchel and swung it over her shoulder. A few feet away, Nancie watched as Wren gathered up a stack of white pages that lay next to the electric typewriter on his dining-room table. He carried them to the built-in wooden buffet and locked them in the top drawer. Next, he dropped the key into the pencil holder above it.

"What kind of class are you two taking?" Nancie asked.

"Creative writing." Risa looked at Wren. "Ready?"

"Ready."

Nancie had to keep her jaw from dropping. "Creative writing? Wren, I didn't know you could write. I didn't know you were even interested in writing."

"He is. And he's really good, too," Risa gushed.

Wren's expression was one of sheer embarrassment. He tried to hide it by kissing the girls good-bye and giving Alexa last-minute instructions.

"Dad, I don't want Mom to stay here," Nancie heard the girl whine under her breath. "Can't I come with you?"

Nancie fought against the billow of hurt and insult that came crashing at her. "Alexa," she all but pleaded, "let's get along tonight, okay? I love you and I don't want bad feelings between us."

Wren muttered something for Alexa's ears only, and she finally nodded in agreement. "Thanks, Nancie," he said, turning toward her. "Make yourself at home."

She summoned a tiny smile. "Sure. Have fun."

Risa told the girls good-bye and left without so much as a backward glance at Nancie.

Wren followed her out and closed the door behind them.

six

By nine o'clock, Alexa had obediently crawled into bed, while Laura lay on the couch, watching a silly video about personified vegetables. Nancie had never seen the likes of it before, but Laura claimed her father deemed it appropriate, so it had to be. Wren was a fanatic about what the girls watched on television—another thing about him that drove Nancie crazy. How would their daughters ever grow up to be worldly-wise if Wren continued to shelter them the way he did?

She expelled an exasperated sigh and took her plate into the kitchen, depositing it in the sink. The lasagna had tasted delicious. At first Nancie had stubbornly decided against eating any, but finally hunger got the best of her.

After rinsing dishes, Nancie ambled into Alexa's bedroom. "Sleep well, honey."

"G'night, Mom."

Nancie smiled and turned away from the partially closed door. She and Alexa had gotten along very well tonight. Finally. A step in the right direction.

Walking back into the living room and passing through the dining area, Nancie paused beside the buffet and stared at the drawer that Wren had locked before he left. What were those papers he'd stuffed inside? Had he lied to her? Was he really seeking custody of the girls? Were those legal briefs?

She glanced at Laura, still engrossed in the video. She looked toward Alexa's room and felt confident that she would stay in bed. Quietly, swiftly, Nancie fished the key out of the pencil holder, then opened the drawer. With deft fingers she removed the pages. One quick scan told her they were typewritten, but not any kind of legal documents.

She began to read, staying close to the open drawer in case Wren should come home. Chapter one. . .

This is a story that Wren's in the process of writing, she soon deduced. It wasn't too bad, either. Perhaps a bit sappy and nothing like the polished literature she was accustomed to reading for her college courses, but it was decent. A guy named George purchased a castle in Germany. . . .

She read to page three and met the character Wren had named "Nan." She bore a striking resemblance to herself, and Nancie wasn't sure if she should feel flattered, insulted, or alarmed. Several pages later, Nancie decided she was definitely offended. Nan was a villainess who thwarted George at every turn, but through it all, he still loved her.

Nancie snorted in disgust. Did Wren really see her as a "Nan"? Did he see himself as the macho character named George?

"You know you love me, Nan," George said. *He captured her in a heated embrace.*

Nancie rolled her eyes.

"Let go of me, you brute. I hate you. I'll always hate you."

"Prove it." George's lips fastened to hers, and just as he presumed, Nan responded to his kiss.

"Oh, good grief," Nancie muttered. "Wren is writing smut!"

She heard the front door open and quickly placed the manuscript back into the drawer, closed, and locked it—all in three smooth moves. Taking a deep breath, she met Wren in the living room. Risa wasn't with him.

"How was class?"

He shrugged. "Okay. How were things here?"

"Fine."

"Really?" Wren looked surprised.

"Really. Alexa and I got along great."

"Glad to hear it."

"I'm glad to report it," Nancie said emphatically. She folded her arms. "Tell me about the creative writing course."

Immediately, Wren appeared uncomfortable. "Nothing really to tell. I registered for it so I could keep myself busy last winter. The class is just about over now."

"Did you meet Risa there?"

He shook his head. "No. We both work at the post office. Risa's the station manager, in fact, but she's the one who talked me into enrolling."

"Do you like it? Writing, I mean. . .do you like writing?"

He gave her a nod before picking up Laura off the couch and setting her feet on the carpeted floor. "Time to get you to bed." Giving Nancie an apologetic glance, he added, "Sorry I'm so late. Risa and I stopped for a cup of coffee."

She arched a brow. "Just friends, huh?"

"Just friends," Wren said with an earnest expression.

"And pigs fly."

He narrowed his gaze. "What do you mean?"

"Do you really expect me to believe you've got a platonic relationship with a woman like her?"

"A woman like her. . . ?"

"Oh, Wren, don't play dumb. Or are you blind? No man in his right mind would ever be content to be 'just friends' with a woman who's got a dynamite figure like Risa's."

"I don't allow myself to look at her figure, and I definitely don't think about it."

"Then what do you do?"

He grinned. "I write."

It was a reply to end all replies; Nancie couldn't think of anything else to say.

"Are you two fighting?" Laura asked, looking worried.

"No, baby. Your mother and I are just discussing something. But you two need to go now. It's past your bedtime."

"Mine, too," Nancie quipped.

Looking over Laura's blond head at her, Wren smiled. "Thanks for helping me out tonight."

"Sure. I owed you one, remember? But if you must know, my motives for staying with the girls tonight were purely selfish. I wanted to spend some time with Alexa."

"That's not selfish, Nancie. That's a mother's heart." Wren helped Laura gather her things and then showed them to the door. "Good night."

He hunkered down in front of Laura, and she hugged him around the neck before they exchanged kisses.

"I love you, Daddy."

"Love you, too, baby."

He straightened, and his brown-eyed gaze bore into Nancie. She held her breath, waiting for him to say he loved her, too.

But he didn't.

"Good night," he said.

" 'Night, Wren." With that Nancie led Laura down the walkway and to her car. She felt oddly disappointed, but immediately told herself that was nonsense. She didn't want Wren to love her. She didn't love him.

Once in the car, she pulled away from the curb and refused to look back.

≥∙

The rest of the week proceeded much like Monday had. Every day after work, Wren picked up the girls. Ruth said she didn't mind that he came two hours early now that the weather was getting nicer. She and her husband, Max, owned a sailboat and liked to spend evenings at the yacht club. The sooner her charges went home, the sooner the Bairds could go to the lake. Wren, too, was happy with the arrangement. He figured the girls would spend ten hours fewer in day care each week, and he would save some money. What's more, he got to spend extra time with his daughters, particularly Laura, and so far, Nancie hadn't balked at the change in routine.

She did surprise Wren, however, by showing up at his front door on Friday evening.

"I thought I'd bring a few more of Alexa's things over,"

Nancie said, handing him a small pink duffle bag.

"Thanks." Wren eyed her curiously. She hadn't been acting like herself for the past few days. "Everything okay? You seem down in the dumps lately. . .depressed."

"It's been a long week."

Wren nodded. He knew what those were like.

"Any plans this weekend?" she asked.

He furrowed his brow in thought. "Nothing special. How 'bout you?"

Nancie shook her head.

"Well, use the time to relax. You said you've been stressed."

"Yeah. . ." Turning, she descended the steps of the worn porch with peeling paint.

"Have a good weekend," he called.

She just sort of waved over her shoulder.

Odd, he thought as he reentered the house.

❧

Nancie's peculiar behavior bothered Wren right up until Saturday afternoon. That's when he remembered: *Tomorrow's Mother's Day!*

"Girls," he called into the backyard, where they were at play with some neighbor kids. "Come on inside a minute."

They did as he asked, and once he had their full attention, Wren announced that they were going shopping for Mother's Day gifts.

"Good thing you remembered, Daddy," Laura said.

"No kidding." Wren wondered how the date had snuck up on him this way, but at least he hadn't missed it altogether. He made a mental note to buy his own mother a gift while he and the girls shopped today. The three of them could visit her tomorrow afternoon—his mother always loved to see the girls.

"Last year Mom was at school," Alexa remarked as they walked to the car.

"That's right," Wren answered. "She took summer classes last year, didn't she?"

Alexa nodded. "I think she likes school more than Laura and me."

"That's not true, Lex," Wren said, opening the car door. "And you've got to stop thinking like that. It hurts your mother when you say those things."

"She says bad things about you," his daughter spouted.

"Like what?" Wren usually discouraged Alexa from tattling, but this time he thought he'd hear her out. Maybe if he allowed her to vent, she'd feel better.

"Mom said it's your fault that you guys are divorced. She said you weren't a good husband. You didn't make her happy."

"I suppose that's partly true."

Alexa's eyes grew wide with indignation. "No, it's not!"

"Look, Lex, I tried my best to please your mom, but I'm sure there are things I could have—should have—done better."

The child's face fell. "But I remember how she yelled at you that one night and told you to leave. I hate it that you and Mom are divorced now."

"I hate it, too. But being angry isn't going to change things."

Alexa cast her gaze at her feet. Wren cupped her chin and forced her to look back at him.

"Your mom needs the Lord. She doesn't know Him like you and Laura do. You need to show her the love of Jesus, and you can't do that if you're angry with her."

Fat tears pooled in the girl's eyes, so Wren pulled her against his chest and kissed the top of her head, rubbing her back consolingly. After several long moments he gave her a gentle squeeze and then steered her into the backseat of the car.

"Better now?"

Alexa nodded, albeit reluctantly, as she wiped her eyes with her palms.

"Good." He closed the door and walked around to the driver's side. Seating himself behind the wheel, he decided he had required that little lecture as much as Alexa. It was a good reminder. They were the "light" Nancie needed to see.

seven

Mother's Day.

Nancie forced herself out of bed, feeling hollow, empty. . . lonely. Knotting the tie of her white satin bathrobe at the waist, she padded to the kitchen and set a pot of coffee to brewing. She figured she had the post-semester blues—similar to the letdown some people experience right after Christmas. She'd been so busy for so long that now she felt isolated, which was especially depressing today.

Wren could have been more sensitive, she inwardly groused. But he obviously hadn't remembered the day's significance—that was evident on Friday night when she'd stopped over. She wondered if he and Risa had plans with the girls, although Nancie really had no evidence on which to base that notion. She'd questioned Laura, who claimed she'd only met the other woman twice—at a picnic last Saturday and then Monday night. Most likely, what Wren had told her about his relationship with Risa was true. But Nancie guessed it wouldn't be long before she'd be hearing about a budding romance, and she secretly envied them.

Coffee in hand, she walked to the door, opened it cautiously, and retrieved her thick Sunday newspaper. She still felt somewhat anxious from last week's mugging. As she made her way to her favorite, most comfortable chair, the doorbell sounded, causing Nancie to jump and spill the steaming liquid in her cup onto the carpet.

"Aw, man. . ." She hurried to the kitchen to fetch some paper towels. On her way back, she paused at the intercom.

"Yes," she answered.

"Happy Mother's Day!" her daughters cried from the lobby.

53

A twinge of guilt assailed her. So Wren had remembered after all. . . .

Nancie buzzed up the girls, and within the time it took her to sponge up the coffee spill, they were knocking at the door. She opened it, and two colorful presents were thrust at her.

"How nice," she said with a smile.

Alexa and Laura entered the apartment, encouraging Nancie to open the gifts.

"We can't stay too long," Alexa added. "Dad is out in the car waiting, and we have to go to church."

"You don't have to, Alexa," Nancie told her. "If you don't want to attend church with your father, he can't force you to go."

"No, Mom," she said, shaking her light brown head, "I do want to go. . .it's just that we have to get going or we'll be late."

Nancie replied with a single nod. Ever since the divorce, Alexa had defended her father. While it didn't irk Nancie any less now than it had in the past eighteen months, she was making a concerted effort to hide her emotions in an attempt to salvage the relationship between herself and her oldest daughter.

"Thanks for the Mother's Day present," Nancie told Alexa, opening hers first. Under the bright, floral-patterned paper, she found a photo album and some film. "Oh, wonderful!"

"I know how you like taking pictures," Alexa said.

"I do. Thanks." Nancie gave her a hug and kiss, thankful the girl allowed it. Perhaps Alexa was working toward harmony between them, too.

She opened Laura's then—a box of chocolate candy and a bottle of bubble bath.

"Thank you, sweetheart."

"Do you like it? Here. . .smell."

Laura unscrewed the cap, and Nancie took a whiff of foaming bath liquid.

"Mmm, nice."

Laura beamed. "All of us can use it, so we smell good."

Nancie chuckled lightly.

"C'mon, Laura, we gotta go," Alexa said. "Dad's waiting."

"Okay."

The girls kissed their mother good-bye, and Nancie thought Alexa seemed sincere with her affection and in wishing her a good Mother's Day. But as she walked them to the door, Nancie's heart sank. Once they left, she'd be alone again. *It's my fault,* she admitted. *I should have planned better. I should have told Wren I was going to switch the schedule so I could have the girls with me today.* Tears of remorse filled her eyes.

"What's wrong, Mumma?" Laura asked, catching a glimpse of her misty eyes.

Nancie quickly blinked her tears away. "Nothing, honey," she fibbed. "You guys have fun today."

"We're going to see Grandma," Alexa said. "Dad bought her one of those jigsaw puzzles she likes."

"I'm sure she'll appreciate that," Nancie replied, remembering how Wren's mother could sit for hours pressing together all those pieces. Simple. That's where Wren got it from, she guessed. But Nancie didn't dislike her former mother-in-law. In fact, they still corresponded from time to time.

After one more kiss and final waves of good-bye, the girls departed. Nancie looked over her gifts again, knowing Wren had most likely paid for them—and had miraculously removed the price tags. Nancie grinned ruefully. After twelve years of Mother's Day presents, he'd finally gotten that part right.

&

"What do you mean she was crying?" Wren inquired after getting Laura's report.

"She's sad, Daddy. I can tell."

"Maybe they were tears of joy because she liked your present so much," Wren suggested.

He looked at Alexa, who just shrugged. No help there.

Shifting his gaze back to Laura, he asked, "You really think she's sad? Should I see if I can find out what's wrong?" Wren knew it wasn't like Nancie to cry. That simply wasn't her style.

In response to his question, the child nodded her blond head vigorously.

"Lex? What do you think?"

Again a noncommittal up-and-down of her slender shoulders. "If you want to, I guess. . ."

Wren thought it over. "All right, you two. . .wait here. I'm going to talk with your mother."

In the small, locked lobby, he rang Nancie's apartment. After he announced himself, she buzzed him upstairs.

"Did one of the girls forget something?" Nancie asked, meeting him at the doorway. She was clad in a low, scoop-necked white nightgown and robe, which caused Wren's mouth to go dry. Suddenly he recalled the unique softness of her body—every freckle, every curve. . . .

Casting his gaze at his feet, he shifted his stance and scratched his jaw uncomfortably. Why did that memory have to surface now?

"Wren?"

"Umm. . ." He forced himself to look into her face—and only there. "Laura said you were crying and I. . .well, I thought I'd make sure you're okay."

She frowned slightly before setting her hands on her hips. "Don't you ever get tired of being a nice guy? Nice guys finish last, don't you know that by now?"

He drew back. "Well, I can see you're just fine," he said, struggling in vain to keep the edge out of his voice. "See ya later."

He turned and headed down the dimly lit hallway.

"Wren, wait. . . . I'm sorry. You didn't deserve that."

He paused and slowly turned back around.

Just then a curious neighbor from across the way poked his gray head out the door and stared at Nancie. She quickly waved Wren inside her apartment, and after he was in, she closed the door soundly.

"That guy is such a busybody. His wife is, too."

Wren didn't reply. He just stood there, still smarting from Nancie's retort about "nice guys."

She walked slowly toward him, and he looked away. Didn't she have any idea what a temptress she was at the moment?

"I've got to get going," he muttered, pulling the car keys from his trouser pocket. He wanted something to hold so he wouldn't be enticed to hold her, although he seriously doubted she'd allow him any such pleasure. She didn't love him anymore. She was fond of saying so. Why couldn't he get that through his thick skull?

"You're nervous," she said.

"The girls are out in the car. I don't want to leave them there too long."

He didn't see Nancie's reaction because he refused to take his eyes off the keys he continued to turn in his palm.

"Wren, I'm sorry for what I said before."

He nodded, although he knew that's what she thought of him. In her book, he definitely was a loser.

"And if you must know, yes, I was crying," she continued. "I don't feel like being without my children on Mother's Day."

Wren sighed wearily. "Nancie. . ."

"I know. It's nobody's fault but mine."

"I won't argue with that," he said sheepishly.

Glancing at her at last, he saw her kind of roll her eyes.

"The girls and I have plans to visit my mother," he began, thinking Nancie expected him to alter his arrangements for her. . .again. He didn't want to, but maybe they could work out a compromise.

"Could I come with you?"

Wren blinked. He couldn't believe what he just heard. "What?"

"Oh, I suppose Risa is riding along, huh? To meet your parents?"

"Risa?" He frowned. "No. She's in Illinois this weekend visiting some friends. I told you, there's nothing going on between Risa and me."

"That's what you think," Nancie smirked. "That woman wants to make a husband out of you, Wren. I could see it in her eyes when she looked at you."

He conceded a slight nod, knowing full well that's exactly what Risa had in mind, even though he tried to tell her it could never be.

Nancie stepped closer to him, finger-combing back her shoulder-length blond hair. "If you let me come with you today, Wren, I promise I'll be nice. For Alexa's sake."

He peered down at her, noting the pert, freckled nose he used to love to kiss. "What about me?" he fairly croaked. "Do you really think I'm without feelings, Nancie? What do you think spending a day with you will do to me?"

"I said I'll be nice."

"Yeah, that's what I'm worried about." He shook his head and stepped around her, making his way to the door; but Nancie caught his elbow.

"Wren, please? My life is a mess right now. My coworkers think I'm a witch just because I haven't gone out of my way to befriend anybody, so I'm trying to change my image at the office. Alexa thinks I hate her, but I'm working on remedying that, too. And I know you and I have been at odds for years, but—"

"Let's get one thing straight," he said, whirling on her. "I was never at odds with you. Everything you wanted, you got. My ambition in life was to please you, Nancie, and you were right when you called me a failure. I failed at making you happy and it still hurts. On the other hand, I admire you for taking note of all the wrongs in your life and trying to set them right. But don't kid yourself. You wouldn't enjoy spending an afternoon with me—even if Alexa and Laura were around."

She let go of his arm and turned away. "You're probably right."

Nodding, he walked the rest of the way to the door. "Treat yourself to lunch, Nancie," he suggested, his hand on the doorknob. "Go shopping."

When no reply came, he stood there scrutinizing her back as she stared out the large living-room windows.

Then he saw her shoulders shake slightly.

"Nancie?" Curiously puzzled, he dropped his keys into his pants pocket and stepped forward. When he reached her, he carefully cupped her upper arm and forced her to face him. Tears were slipping from her eyes. "No way," he said in disbelief. "I haven't seen you cry since your mother died."

She practically dissolved in his hands. Soon she was in his arms.

"Oh, Wren, I think I'm having a nervous breakdown," she sobbed against his shoulder. "It started after I got jumped last Sunday night. I haven't been able to sleep. I'm anxious. I'm depressed. Maybe I need professional help."

"Maybe you need the Lord," he replied, stroking her silky hair and reveling in the feeling of holding her body close to his. He felt a little guilty for finding any pleasure in her pain, but hadn't this been what he'd been praying for—for God to soften Nancie's heart?

"I just don't want to be alone today," she said with a sniff. Pulling her chin back, she glanced at his shirt before giving him an apologetic smile. "By the way, I slobbered all over your nice, clean Oxford."

Wren shrugged. It seemed a small price to pay for what had just occurred.

Nancie lifted an inquiring brow. "Can you finally iron your own shirts without scorching them?"

He shook his head and grinned. "Alexa irons them for me."

"Wren!"

"Well, she likes to," he said in his own defense. "She irons every Saturday night while Laura cooks supper."

"What?" Nancie backed out of his embrace. "You allow a seven-year-old to use the stove?"

"I'm usually right there." Sensing an argument on the rise, Wren made for the door. "Still want to come this afternoon?" he called over his shoulder.

A pause.

He swung around and lifted an expectant brow.

"Yes," Nancie replied, looking like a lost little girl as she continued to stand by the window.

"You can't try to pick a fight with me," he warned her halfheartedly.

"I won't," she promised, and Wren almost chuckled. She resembled Laura after a thorough reprimand.

"Okay," he acquiesced. "I'll pick you up after church. . . around noon."

Nancie nodded.

"Have you got a Bible around here?"

"Probably."

"Well," he said, opening the door, "if you've got time, read the Psalms. They'll soothe your soul better than any psychologist."

"Yeah, sure," she replied skeptically. "But I'll be ready at noon."

Wren left the apartment, and for the first time in a very, very long while, there was an airiness to his step and a swell of hope in his heart.

eight

Risa approached Wren as he prepared to leave for the day. "Did you have a good weekend?" she called from several feet away.

He smiled upon seeing her, and Risa's heart soared. "Yeah. How 'bout you?"

"Good. I spent time with some friends I hadn't seen in a long while."

"That's always nice."

Risa nodded and folded her arms. "What did you do?"

"Well, Saturday was pretty much an ordinary day," he replied, leaning up against a nearby doorjamb as they stood conversing in the back room. "Sunday after church," he continued, "I took the girls to visit my mother, who lives about an hour and a half north of here, and my ex-wife came along."

"She did?" Risa felt her eyes grow wide.

"Uh-huh. Nancie was on her best behavior, too." He chuckled lightly.

"I don't understand you, Wren. From what you've told me, it sounds like your ex has been extremely selfish throughout your marriage. She took you to the cleaners when she divorced you. She's mean and condescending. How can you act civil toward her, let alone spend an afternoon with her?"

He shrugged and his smile faded. "Nancie's going through a hard time right now, and I feel obligated as a Christian to be there for her."

"You're too good to be true," Risa declared with a wag of her head.

"No, I'm not. You just don't know me very well."

She grinned. "I know you well enough. . . . Say, are you

going to class tonight?"

"Sure am. Are you?"

Risa nodded.

"Nancie said she'd stay with the girls again."

"Great." Risa took a step closer. "Can I bring dinner over like I did last week?"

"I don't know if that's a good idea," he said, growing serious. "Risa, I don't want you to foster any hope that—"

"Not to worry," she cut in. "We're just friends. But I happen to have a taste for veal parmigiana, and I hate to cook just for myself. Besides, Wren, I'm Italian. I love to feed people. You and the girls have to eat, right? Sounds like a match to me."

"Only if it's a platonic one," he quipped.

"Right."

Wren cracked a smile. "Veal parmigiana, huh?"

"I make the best."

"You drive a hard bargain, Risa. You caught me at a weak moment. I'm starved."

She laughed. "I just have to take care of a few things and then I'll come over to your place."

Wren gave her a parting smile before leaving the postal station.

Watching him go, Risa felt a bittersweet pang. While she might access Wren's kitchen this evening, she still hadn't gained entry to his heart.

❧

The woman could definitely cook—Nancie had to give her that much. Never in her life had she tasted such a delicious meal.

"I think you should marry her, Wren," Nancie whispered to him as she carried several plates in from the dining room. They were alone in the kitchen, and he stood at the sink, washing the dishes. "You'd never starve to death."

He sort of smirked, but didn't look up from the silverware in his hands.

"Why don't you marry her?" Nancie asked, seriously now. She couldn't help it. She didn't understand him. Risa was gorgeous and obviously smitten with him. Wasn't Wren human?

"I don't love her," he stated simply.

A flash caught her eye, and she spied the wedding ring he continued to wear on his left hand. "Wren, we're divorced. You're free to pursue a relationship with Risa."

He finally glanced at her, shook the water off his hands, and reached for the dish towel. "Thanks for giving me your permission," he stated with a note of sarcasm. "But Risa and I are just friends, and that's the way I want it to stay."

"Why?"

"Because I personally believe God gave me one shot at marriage, and I blew it."

"Don't be so hard on yourself. Besides, chances are you wouldn't blow it a second time."

After a noncommittal shrug of his broad shoulders, he began drying and putting away the dishes. His lack of response irked her for some reason, and Nancie shook her head at him before leaving the kitchen. She found Risa in the dining room, clearing the rest of the table. Nancie picked up a few glasses.

"He's a lost cause," she told the flaming-haired woman. "Don't waste your time."

"I assume you're speaking about Wren."

"Uh-huh. He's behind the times. I can't imagine what you see in him."

"You want to know what I see?" Risa countered. "I see a wonderful, chivalrous, caring man who stands by his word."

"I've got firsthand news for you, honey. Chivalry is boring."

"And I've got firsthand news for you. Chivalry is refreshing. There aren't many decent men left in this world."

Risa walked into the kitchen, leaving Nancie to mull over the reply. Finally, she gave up and decided it was all relative. In the same way that one man's junk was another's treasure,

Nancie supposed one woman's ex-husband could be another's knight in shining armor.

Well, she can have him, she thought cynically. *I certainly don't want him.*

Nancie strolled into the living room, where Laura sat reading a book and Alexa struggled through her math homework. She heard Risa's voice above the din of rushing tap water in the kitchen, and then Wren chuckled at whatever she'd just said. They'd make a good couple, Wren and Risa. Even their names sounded harmonic.

Nancie took a seat beside Alexa and offered to help her.

"No, that's okay, Mom."

She looked across the room at Laura and realized her daughters were growing up fast. Both had been in their glory tonight, helping Risa prepare dinner.

Her mind wandered. *Suppose Wren did indeed marry her. . . would Alexa and Laura want to live with them?* The thought sent a shiver of apprehension up Nancie's spine. If that happened, she'd truly be alone—and solitude was something she'd begun to fear lately. She never imagined herself growing old all by herself, and she certainly wasn't getting any younger.

Shaking off her melancholy, Nancie glanced at Alexa. "Are you enjoying living with your father?"

She nodded.

Nancie noticed Laura's wistful gaze. "Don't tell me you want to live with him, too?"

The child shrugged and turned back to her book.

"Okay," she said, exasperated. "Explain to me why it's so much better over here. Our apartment is nicer."

"We still love you, Mumma," Laura stated with a diplomatic air. "It's just that Daddy needs us."

Arching a questioning brow, Nancie looked back at Alexa. "Is that right?"

"I don't know," her oldest said, keeping her gaze on her arithmetic.

"I understand you iron his shirts and Laura cooks."

A tiny smile peeped out from Alexa's otherwise stony expression.

"You can iron and cook at our apartment, too, you know," Nancie offered glibly.

Before further comment could be made, Wren and Risa entered the room.

"We've got to leave or we'll be late for class," Wren announced. He bent over, cupped Laura's small face in his hands, and kissed her soundly.

"Bye, Daddy," she said, smiling up at him adoringly.

"Lex, get your homework done and I'll check it when I get back."

She nodded, before lifting her chin and puckering her lips to receive Wren's fatherly smooch.

He glanced at Nancie. "Want a kiss, too?"

"No, that's quite all right," she assured him, unable to keep from smiling.

"I'll take one," Risa interjected, a teasing grin on her face.

Wren swung around and laughed. "Out," he demanded lightheartedly, pointing to the front door. "Get going. We're going to be late."

Risa waved to the children and did as she had been asked.

After he had followed her out of the house, Laura looked over and with a most earnest expression, said, "You should have taken the kiss, Mumma."

&

George found himself in a quandary. He couldn't help but love Nan, except the captivating Lucia was working her feminine wiles on him again. Her soft-spoken, uplifting words were like a salve after Nan's hatefully spewed sentiments. The woman could be as cruel as she was determined.

Nancie felt her ire on the rise as she continued to read through the third chapter of Wren's silly novel. Cruel? Is that what he thought of her in real life? But a few pages later, the story took an abrupt turn, and her indignation dissolved as she lost herself in the action. She chuckled inwardly when George heroically saved Nan from a raging fire in her apartment building before rescuing other tenants. In response, Nan agreed to fly to Germany with George and give him an estimate on decorating the castle he'd bought.

She resumed reading.

George smiled to himself. Nan had thought being trapped in a raging inferno was horrifying, but she hadn't yet even come close to knowing the true meaning of the word. His dark, spooky castle, with its surrounding moat, wouldn't allow her to escape its confines. Once she was inside, Nan would have nowhere to run when the shadows frightened her. . .except into his arms.

"Oh, brother," Nancie muttered. However, she had to admit to feeling thoroughly amused and somewhat intrigued. She wanted to know what would happen next.

She glanced over her shoulder to make sure she hadn't disturbed Laura, who had fallen asleep on the couch. Laura continued to doze peacefully.

She flipped over the page and begin reading chapter four.

The flight to Germany was enjoyable. George and Nan got along surprisingly well, which pleased their two beautiful daughters. At the last minute, George had decided to take them along.

She continued to pore over the manuscript and decided the scene smacked of their Mother's Day outing yesterday afternoon. *Wren must have written this part last night.* She'd already noticed that when she and Wren were on friendly terms, so were George and Nan. When they weren't, Lucia began sounding more like the heroine of the story. This was obviously a cathartic project for Wren—and he'd all but admitted as much last week.

Suddenly she heard the front door open. She hurriedly tucked the loose pages into the drawer where she'd found them. It hadn't been locked tonight.

"Hi," he said, entering the living room and setting down his book bag. "Everything go all right?"

"I'm not the sixteen-year-old baby-sitter, Wren," she said facetiously, "so you can spare me the interrogation."

He grinned. "Sorry."

She smiled. "How was your writing class?"

"Good. But I'm dying of thirst." He headed for the kitchen, and Nancie followed.

"I noticed you have an old electric typewriter. Is that what you type your assignments on?" She knew it was, but wanted to see if he'd tell her about his novel. Maybe then she wouldn't feel quite so guilty for reading it.

"Yep. I bought that machine at the Salvation Army store for fifty bucks." He took a healthy swig out of the orange juice container.

"Wren, that's gross. Use a glass." To his curious look, she shrugged. "Forget I said that. This is your house."

"Thank you."

"Why don't you buy a computer? That would make your life simpler."

"Can't afford it right now."

"Oh."

He put the carton back into the fridge and closed the door.

"Do you write other things? Articles for the newspaper. . . anything like that?"

"Yeah, I fool around a little."

"Will you let me read something you wrote?"

Wren shook his dark brown head. "Nope."

"Why?"

"Because I'm not very good, Nancie. This is just a little hobby for me. Kind of like my mother and her jigsaw puzzles."

She opened her mouth, preparing to refute him, but closed it again. She had wanted to tell him he wasn't a bad writer, but she could hardly say such a thing without confessing to snooping.

"I think it's really neat that you've taken up writing," she said carefully. "I'm actually quite impressed."

"You are?"

Nancie nodded.

He stepped closer, then stopped, and stood before her with arms akimbo. Looking up at him, Nancie decided that Wren was still a nice-looking man. She could understand Risa's attraction. A warmth suddenly entered his dark gaze, a response that Nancie recognized.

"Wren, I don't want you to love me anymore."

His dark eyes briefly clouded with anguish. But a moment later, it was gone. "I can't help it. We were married for a long time. My feelings for you are deep-rooted and won't go away just because you changed your mind."

"Fall in love with Risa and be happy."

He narrowed his gaze. "Something tells me you wouldn't really like it if I did."

She arched a challenging brow. "I just suggested it, didn't I? Do you think I say things I don't mean?"

"Uh-huh."

Her palm itched to slap the smirk off his face. But before the thought could become a reality, the unthinkable happened. He backed her up against the kitchen counter and kissed her.

"Wren!" she cried in utter surprise. She gave him a shove, which didn't budge him. "Stop it. You're acting stupid." She thought he was behaving like his George character, and Nancie couldn't quite believe it.

Leaning toward her, he gently grabbed her resisting arms and kissed her temple, her cheek, her neck.

"Knock it off, Wren."

"You really want me to?" he whispered close to her ear.

She hesitated—why, she would never know. But it was all the encouragement he needed. In a heartbeat, Nancie found herself wrapped in his arms with Wren's lips slowly gliding across hers.

"Mom? Dad?"

The spell was broken.

Nancie came to her senses in a flash and pushed on Wren's chest. He moved away easily.

"Now you did it!" she hissed.

Wren turned around, and they both saw Alexa standing in the doorway leading from the hall. Her confused expression said it all; however, the question still tumbled from her lips.

"What are you doing?"

"We're not arguing, Lex," Wren said, a touch of amusement in his voice.

She looked from one to the other, obviously still uncertain.

"It's all right, Alexa," Nancie told her. "Go back to bed. Laura and I were just leaving." She shot Wren a look of derision before marching into the living room.

Within moments, she had Laura up and ready to go. Wren saw them to the door.

"If you're expecting an apology out of me, forget it," he said.

Nancie didn't reply. In truth, she felt as baffled as Alexa had looked. She had enjoyed that little tryst in the kitchen.

But she shouldn't have. They were divorced. There was nothing between them anymore.

"Good night, Nancie," he said after walking them out to the car and helping to situate Laura in the backseat.

" 'Night," she replied in a voice as crisp as the cold, damp wind.

But as she pulled away from the curb, she couldn't help but release a tiny laugh. There wasn't a doubt in her mind that next week she'd be reading this scene in Wren's book.

nine

"Kissing in the kitchen?" Ruth Baird giggled like a high school girl a few days later. Nancie bristled. "Alexa told me all about it."

"I'm sure she did," Nancie retorted. "I'm going to have to talk to that girl."

"Any chance of you and Wren getting back together? I know that's been his prayer."

"None—and prayers don't work on me. I'm not a religious person."

"Well, that's good."

Nancie blinked, suddenly puzzled. "Good? I thought you were one of those born again people. . .like Wren."

"I am. But being born again isn't about religion. It's about having a relationship with the Lord Jesus Christ."

"Oh, right. Wren's told me that before."

"Did you ever listen?"

Nancie nodded. "One night I heard him out. I let him show me some Bible verses about sin and hell and how God sent His Son to die for us. But I just don't believe it. I'm an intellect, Ruth. I think all the religions of the world have merit. I find that studying them is fascinating. And you know what's interesting about it all? Each religion claims to be the right and only source of truth."

"But obviously that's not possible, so you have to choose which god you'll serve."

"Or choose no specific god at all, which is what I've done." Nancie glanced at her watch. She had to leave or she'd be late for work. "Ruth, look, I'm into the human experience. I believe that when we die, we'll each go to our own kind of heaven. You and I will have our own unique places in the universe."

"All by ourselves?" Ruth asked with a frown. "That doesn't sound like something to look forward to. I don't want to spend an eternity alone. There's no hope in that.

"My God says I'll share heaven with all His other children," she continued with a wistful expression. "We'll sing and rejoice together and worship the Lord Jesus Christ, free from the worries of this world."

"To each his own," Nancie replied, making her way to the door. "Have a good day, Ruth."

"You, too."

Walking to her car, Nancie felt rocked to the core. She'd never thought of it before. . .spending an eternity alone. That's the last thing she wanted!

But I won't be alone, she thought, squelching the anxiety that had quickened her pulse. *I'll be part of the universe. The moon. The sun. The stars.*

Driving away from the curb, Nancie put a firm halt on her musings. She didn't want to think about death and eternity— not when she had so much to live for!

❧

"Lex, I'm going to play basketball tonight with some of the guys from church. . .and guess what?"

"I have to come along," she replied with little enthusiasm.

"Right. You win the prize!" Wren chuckled.

Alexa rolled her eyes, but smiled all the same.

"Bring your homework if you'd like."

"No. I'll do it when I get back home."

Wren looked at her askance. "Do you think of this as 'home,' Lex? Or do you feel like you have two homes?"

The girl began her reply with a habitual shrug. "To me, there's Mom's home and this home. . .the one I like best."

"Why's that?" Wren probed, pulling on his spring jacket.

"It's got the furniture in it that I remember from our

house on Cramer Street."

"Mm, I see." Wren knew that Alexa didn't like change and the divorce had really thrown her. She'd struggled in school for the past year, but had finally worked hard enough to get her grades back up. Now it seemed she was on the emotional mend, surrounded by things that comforted her—things that Nancie had discarded after she'd sold the house. However, there was something else Wren wanted to see happen in his daughter's life. "Lex, you can be happy anywhere—here, at your mother's apartment, or on the mission field, if God calls you there. You can be content wherever you live. You've got His Holy Spirit in you. You're saved by grace, but now you need to learn how to lean on the Lord and depend on Him. He's the only one who can help you roll with the punches—and, trust me, life comes with plenty of them."

She didn't answer, but Wren felt confident that she would at least think it over.

"Dad, are you and Mom going to get back together?"

Wren was momentarily taken aback by the shift in conversation. "I don't know," he said at last.

"She can't really hate you if she had her arms around you and was kissing you."

The grin on his face refused to be stifled, although he couldn't quite believe what had taken place in his kitchen—and he was even more surprised by the fact that he'd initiated the whole thing. "We'll keep praying, okay, Lex?"

She nodded.

"But there is something that would have to happen before your mom and I could get back together," Wren added, serious now. "She would have to become a Christian. Otherwise our marriage would be just as bad as before. . .maybe worse."

"Great. . . That'll never happen," Alexa muttered.

"God can do anything," Wren quickly reminded her. "He saved me, didn't He?"

Wearing her usual indifferent expression, Alexa shrugged.

Together they left the house, pausing on the front porch long enough for Wren to lock the door. Then Alexa pulled on his jacket sleeve.

"Dad, look who's here. . . ."

He turned to see Risa running through the rain from her car. She expelled an audible sigh once she reached them.

"This weather's incredible. It's been storming all week long!"

"Tell me about it," Wren replied. "I've walked my route in this stuff."

"As the station manager," Risa said, lifting her chin and giving herself a look of importance, "I'll be sure to note that in your file and recommend you for a wage increase."

"Promises, promises."

She laughed, and Wren joined her. Alexa watched curiously.

"Where are you guys off to?" Risa wanted to know. Tendrils of wavy red hair were rain-plastered to the side of her face.

"Dad's playing basketball in the gym at our church."

"Oh, I'd like to see that," Risa said with an impish grin.

"Good. You can keep me company, 'cause Dad's making me go."

Wren felt that his fate had just been sealed. No point in arguing about it, either—he'd never win. "All right, come on. . . ."

They stepped off the porch and walked briskly down the cement walkway. Just as they reached the car, Nancie pulled up to the curb and rolled down the window of her vehicle. She glanced at Wren before surveying his entourage.

"I have some shopping to do," she said, "and I wondered if Alexa wanted to come along."

Wren looked over at his daughter, who shook her head.

"You mean you'd prefer to watch your old man shoot hoops than spend money, Lex? What's wrong with you?"

She responded with a laugh and climbed into the car.

Wren gave Nancie a bewildered look. "I'll never figure

out a woman's mind."

"Nope, probably not," she replied. "Where you going?"

"To play basketball with some friends. Lex and Risa are coming as spectators."

"Really? Well, in that case, Mr. Michael Jordan, how about taking Laura with you? She doesn't feel like shopping."

His youngest peered at him from the backseat. "Please, Daddy, can I come with you?"

"Sure, come on," he agreed.

Laura was out of Nancie's car and into his in a matter of moments.

"What time will you be through?"

"Maybe nine," Wren replied.

"Oh. . .well, I won't be shopping for that long. Where are you playing?"

"At the church."

Nancie nodded. "Okay, I'll pick Laura up there."

"It's a date," he said without really thinking about it.

She did a double take, casting him an annoyed look in the process, before driving off.

Way to go, he admonished himself. Nancie acted as though she hadn't forgiven him for taking such liberties in his kitchen, and now he had to go and mention the subject of dating, even if it had been in fun. No doubt he'd fueled her fiery temper. *I can be such an idiot.*

Getting into his car, he started the engine. "Everyone ready?"

"All set," Risa said from the passenger seat beside him. "I can't wait to see you play. I'll bet you're a very good ball player."

"Well, I don't know. . . ." He glanced at her and she smiled back; Wren noted the ardent gleam in her eyes. "I guess I'm not too bad."

❧

The rain came down in sheets. Nancie began to wonder if it would ever stop. The whole week had been like this, some storms generating enough water to flood underpasses and highways. Tonight's weather seemed to be particularly intense. The wind tore through the treetops, and newly budded branches littered the streets and lawns as she drove away from the shopping mall.

Reaching the church, Nancie ran from her car and into the building. She knew where to find the gymnasium, since Wren had been a member of this particular congregation for the past five years. As she neared her destination, the sounds of a bouncing basketball and athletic shoes squeaking on the polished floor grew louder, as did the grunts, groans, and cheers of the six male players. She cast them a quick glance before making her way to the wooden bleachers where Risa sat watching the game; Alexa and Laura were fooling around down at the other end.

"Are we having fun yet?" Nancie asked Risa facetiously.

She smiled slightly and turned back to the ball game. "I'm enjoying myself. Did you have fun shopping?"

Nancie sat down beside her. "I don't know if I'd call it fun, but I found what I needed." Following Risa's gaze, she saw Wren—dressed in navy nylon wind pants and a red T-shirt—preparing to shoot. A moment later, the ball swished through the hoop.

"Nice shot, Wren!" Risa shouted encouragingly.

"Go, Dad!" Alexa called from the far end of the bleachers.

Laura jumped up and down. "Yea!"

Nancie rolled her eyes. "Wren's head is going to get so big, he'll never get it through the gymnasium doorway tonight."

Risa regarded her thoughtfully for several long moments. "You know what I wish?" she finally said. "I wish you'd get out of Wren's life forever."

"Excuse me?" Nancie couldn't believe what she'd just heard.

"I know your kind," Risa went on. "You're a user and

abuser of sweethearted guys like Wren. You're only nice to him when it serves your purposes, otherwise you tear him down every chance you get."

Nancie lofted a brow. "It's none of your business what I do." She eyed the red-haired woman speculatively. "At least now I know where Alexa got her hateful attitude toward me."

"Not a chance," Risa replied with an amused grin. "You can't pin that one on me. Alexa is an intelligent girl. She sees you for what you are—a selfish, self-seeking individual who gives little or no thought to others."

Nancie stood and called for Laura. She wasn't about to stay and listen to any more of this nonsense. As her youngest collected her spring coat, Nancie almost smirked. She ought to tell Risa about how Wren kissed her the other night and said he'd always love her. The twit was wasting her time; Wren wasn't interested in her.

At that moment Wren walked over to the bleachers, accompanied by a dark-haired man.

"What's going on?" he asked, looking concerned.

"Ask your girlfriend," Nancie replied tersely. Grabbing Laura's hand, she left the gym and headed for home.

ten

"I'm sorry, Wren," Risa said. "I couldn't help it."

He shoved his hands into the pockets of his wind pants and stared at his gym shoes. Risa could tell he was disappointed in her for spouting off to his ex-wife. The guy beside him looked somewhat concerned, too, which only increased Risa's discomfort.

"Well, look, what's done is done," the man said. "God can use this, too."

"Sorry," Risa stated once more.

Wren looked up, sent her a wink, and her insides began to quiet. He wasn't angry with her.

She turned and considered the other man. He stood a few inches shorter than Wren and had thick, jet black hair and a dark five-o'clock shadow covering his jaw. His white T-shirt was stained with perspiration from his efforts on the basketball court. "Who's your friend?"

"I guess it's my turn to apologize," Wren said. "I should have introduced you guys. Risa, this is Mike Gerardi. Mike, meet Risa Vitalis."

"It's a pleasure," he replied, sticking out his right hand.

Risa gave it a shake. "Same here."

Folding his arms across his wide chest, Mike frowned. "Vitalis. Hey, you aren't related to Alphonso Vitalis, are you?"

Risa searched her memory. "Does he have a brother named Joseph and a sister, Marie?"

"Yeah, that's him."

"He's my father's cousin." Risa chuckled. "Aren't all of us Italians related somehow?"

"I suppose so," he said with a charming grin. "Alphonso is

a good friend of my family's."

Risa nodded politely before turning her attention back to Wren.

Mike did the same. "So, you think your ex will start World War III now, or what?"

"Your guess is as good as mine," Wren replied. "Nancie is unpredictable."

"Kinda like this weather," Mike remarked as thunder rumbled. It was loud enough to be audible in the gym. Moments later, the lights flickered.

Risa held her tongue. She would have liked to comment on Nancie Nickelson's "stormy" personality, but figured she'd done enough damage for one night.

"Want to get going?" Wren asked her.

She nodded, but sensed it was really his wish.

"Hey, nice to meet you, Risa," Mike called as she departed with Wren and Alexa.

"Back at you," she replied over her shoulder.

Silence filled the car on the way back to Wren's place. Risa thought about apologizing again, but figured it wouldn't do any good. What was done was done.

When they arrived at his duplex, Wren killed the engine. Tossing the keys into the backseat where Alexa caught them, he instructed his daughter to go into the house ahead of him. He'd be there shortly. Once the child was safely inside, Risa figured she was about to get a good lecture—or a sermon. Either way, she probably deserved it. Ruefully, she stared straight ahead at the rain streaming down the windshield. Wren did the same, and for a long while, neither uttered a sound.

Finally, Risa cracked.

"Okay. Go ahead. Yell at me. Tell me what a horrible person I am for telling your ex-wife just exactly what I think of her. Just say something, Wren."

"That's just it. I don't know what to say, except I feel like we should talk."

"You're angry with me."

"Not at all." He turned and looked at her with those deep brown eyes of his and Risa's heart melted. "I'm just worried about you."

"Me?" She had to laugh. "What are you worried about?"

"I think you're taking our relationship too seriously."

"What, you never went to bat for a friend before, Wren?" she questioned. "You never stuck your neck out for someone you cared about?"

"Sure, I've done that."

"I know you have." Risa touched the back of his hand, then slipped her fingers in between his. Wren didn't pull away. "But you're right. I do take our relationship seriously." She paused. "The truth is, I'm in love with you. I can't help it."

Beneath the glow of the streetlights outside the car, she saw him wince. Then he withdrew his hand.

"I know what you're going to say," she continued. "You're about to tell me that you don't feel the same way I do. But Wren. . .can't you at least give me a chance?"

"I probably would if it weren't for my faith," he said, both hands gripping the steering wheel, his gaze set dead ahead.

"What do you mean?"

"We don't share the same beliefs, Risa. I'm a born-again Christian. You're not. Besides, I'm convinced that God only gave me one shot at marriage."

"Some God you have. Doesn't He want you to be happy?"

"Yes. But He wants me to be happy with the woman He ordained to be my wife before the beginning of time."

"Her? Your ex-wife?"

Wren nodded.

"Like I said. . .some God you have. That woman is mean and selfish and brings you nothing but misery. Remember the night we stopped for coffee after class and you described your marriage? It didn't sound like 'happily ever after' to me. You said you tried to please Nancie, but she was never satisfied.

You bought her a house in Shorewood, but it wasn't prestigious enough. She wanted Whitefish Bay. You work hard and earn a decent living, but that wasn't good enough for her, either. Then she divorced you and took everything. She still gets a chunk of your salary and then she makes you pay for child care, among other things. Now she drives a cute foreign sports car and you drive this old thing."

"I know, it doesn't seem fair." Wren sighed. "But the fact is, our failed marriage is as much my fault as Nancie's."

"Whatever." Irritated and feeling more than a little hurt, Risa opened the door and climbed out. Cold raindrops pelted her, but she didn't care.

"Risa, wait."

She ignored Wren's request and strode purposely for her car, parked across the quiet street. Pulling her keys out of her purse, she unlocked the door.

Wren caught her elbow. "Please, Risa, will you let me explain all this? Can I show you from the Bible what God told me? I'd like to hear what you have to say after reading the passages."

She looked up into his beseeching eyes. Rain dripped from his hair, nose, and chin. In just those few moments, they'd both been soaked to the skin.

"Well, I suppose I could come in for a while," she said before giving him a seductive smile. She stepped closer. "Maybe I should get out of these wet clothes. Got something black and slinky?"

"I've got some black sweats. I don't know how 'slinky' they'll be, though."

Risa shook her head. "Sweats aren't what I had in mind, Wren."

"Yeah, I know." He cleared his throat. "Come on. Let's get out of this rain."

She followed him up to the porch and into the house, deciding that if she wanted to spend time with Wren, she'd have to do it on his terms. . .for now. At least he wasn't completely brushing her off.

True to his word, he provided her with a pair of clean sweatpants and a sweatshirt. He even found a pair of thick white athletic socks for her feet. He threw her wet things into the dryer. Then, while Alexa pored over her math book at the dining-room table, Wren opened his Bible in the living room. Risa did her best to cozy up beside him on the couch, but had a feeling he didn't even notice.

"First things first," he said, flipping through the pages reverently. "I want to show you some verses in the book of Romans. Do you know who the apostle Paul was?"

Risa nodded. "I was raised Catholic."

"Okay. Then you're familiar with him and the Bible." He looked at her askance. "Do you believe this book?"

She shrugged. "I pretty much gave up religion altogether after what my stepfather did to me. He used to attend mass every day, but I can tell you there was nothing holy about that guy—or his disgusting friends!"

"Risa, anyone can attend any kind of church and still be as lost as an atheist. Church doesn't save one's soul—Jesus Christ does. Here, look. . . ."

Wren pointed to a verse and read, " 'For all have sinned and fall short of the glory of God.' " He turned a couple of pages and read aloud another verse. " 'For the wages of sin is death, but the gift of God is eternal life in Christ Jesus our Lord.' " He lifted his gaze to hers. "See, none of us is good enough to get to heaven on our own. All of us fall short of God's glory. We all deserve eternal punishment in hell. That's what the Bible is saying here. But if we want eternal life, there is a way to get it. God provided the way. All we have to do is accept His free gift of salvation."

"Okay," Risa said a bit hesitantly, "and what is that 'gift'?"

"God's Son, Jesus Christ."

"He died on the cross for the whole world."

"Right, but His sacrifice was not a generic one-size-fits-all deal. He's a personal Savior, and Christ died for your sins and mine. We sent Him to the cross, Risa."

Shifting uncomfortably, she didn't particularly care for the idea that she was a "sinner," except she knew she wasn't perfect, either. She'd made her share of mistakes. "All right. I agree. I've sinned. So how do I 'accept' Jesus Christ? Go to mass, confession, pray on my rosary five times a day?"

Wren shook his head and grinned. "All you do is confess to God that you're a sinner in need of salvation. God's salvation, not the ones created by man. Then invite Jesus into your heart. Ask Him to share your life. He will."

Risa dropped her head back and laughed. "That's it? Give me a break!"

"That's it. Salvation is a simple thing—so simple, it confounds the wisest of men."

Risa still wasn't convinced, so Wren turned a few more pages of his Bible and pointed out yet another verse. " 'Everyone who calls on the name of the Lord will be saved.' "

"And then what happens? Will I have to do what God wants instead of what I want?"

Wren shook his dark brown head. It still looked damp from the rain. "You don't have to do anything, Risa. But you'll want to please God. He changes His children from the inside out, not the other way around."

"What if God doesn't want me to get married?"

"If you want to get married someday," Wren replied, smiling slightly, "then my guess is God put that desire in your heart. But you've got to be open to His choice of a husband. The man you select might not be the best one for you."

Risa nodded knowingly. They'd come full circle. "You're telling me that you aren't the man God wants for me, right? But how do you know?"

"Good question." Once more, Wren skipped over several more pages in his Bible. The next passage he showed her was highlighted with a yellow marker. "This verse is found in the book of 1 Corinthians, chapter seven. It also was written by the apostle Paul. It says, 'A wife must not separate from her husband. But if she does, she must remain unmarried or else be reconciled to her husband. And a husband must not divorce his wife.' "

"You didn't divorce your ex-wife," Risa argued. "She divorced you."

"Right. But look at this. . . ." Wren had to search out the next set of verses which, moments later, he found in the gospel of Luke. Again he'd highlighted a portion of the text in yellow. "This is what the Savior said, 'Anyone who divorces his wife and marries another woman commits adultery, and the man who marries a divorced woman commits adultery.' "

"But, Wren, I'm not a divorcée!" Risa exclaimed, unable to understand.

"But I am," he replied softly. "You can't marry me. Besides, Nancie might have taken the initiative, but I agreed to the divorce. For all intents and purposes, I divorced her, too.

"Look," he added patiently, "I know there are a lot of Christians who've been through the whole process. I have friends who have been divorced and are now happily remarried. I in no way stand in judgment of them. All I know is, it wouldn't be right for me to remarry. God used this verse in Scripture to tell me that."

Tears of discouragement filled Risa's eyes. She looked away. "You're a puzzle, Wren Nickelson."

"To a lot of people I am, that's true." He closed his Bible. "And now I'll really blow you away by admitting that I'm still in love with my wife."

"Ex-wife," Risa reminded him. "And I'm not the least surprised to hear it, either. But you're too good for her."

In the dining room, Alexa had twisted around in her chair and now sat watching on curiously. Risa felt all the more frustrated. She'd forgotten the girl was nearby.

Wren obviously had forgotten, too. "Lex, are you done with your homework?"

She nodded.

"Then get yourself ready for bed."

Disappointment crossed her small face, but she did as her father instructed.

"I'd better get going," Risa said, rising from the couch. "Can I return your clothes tomorrow at work?"

"Sure. Let me go downstairs and get yours out of the dryer."

"Forget it, Wren. Just bring them with you in the morning."

He nodded agreeably and stood by while she removed the thick socks she'd borrowed and stepped into her leather flats.

"I won't make the cover of *Vanity Fair* in this outfit," she quipped, feeling self-conscious now on top of all her other tumultuous emotions.

He just smiled and politely saw her to the door.

With one hand on the knob, she turned to face him again. "I'm still not giving up on you—us." She saw his gaze soften, and she loved him all the more for it. "You're the most wonderful man I've ever met."

"There's a slew of guys better than me out there, Risa. But your first love needs to be the Lord Jesus Christ before you'll ever find a man here on earth who will make you happy."

She didn't believe him. She didn't understand. Pulling open the door, she turned and walked into the drenching, bitter rain.

๛

Nancie had almost secured a date for Saturday night. Deciding that the redheaded hussy had been right when she'd said Nancie should get out of Wren's life forever, she strove to make new friends at work and build a future of her own. She'd gone so far as to request that Wren leave Laura at the Bairds' instead of taking her to his place every day after work. He complied and, as a result, Nancie hadn't seen him in more than a week. She didn't stay with the girls on Monday night so that he could attend his writing class, and she'd all but convinced herself that she couldn't care less about Wren's goofy novel.

With that said and done, she'd set her sights on Pete Larsen. Ironically, he, too, was a redhead, although his shade was darker than Risa's, more auburn than carrot orange. Nancie could tell he'd been attracted to her since his first day on the job—the day after Nancie was mugged. Pete had even pursued her after his colleagues had dubbed her a "blond broomstick rider" in the cafeteria. However, once he learned she had children, his interest evaporated.

"It's not like the girls have to come with us," Nancie had stated in her own defense. "They stay with their father on weekends. And this is only a date, for pity's sake!"

"I know," Pete replied. "But I don't want to get tangled up with a woman who has kids."

"You don't like kids?"

"Yeah, I do. . .just not some other guy's kids. Been there, done that, Nancie. Your daughters would most likely hate me because they're devoted to their dad, and it ultimately would affect our relationship, so let's not even go there."

"Fine." She tried to hide her hurt feelings and disappointment as she left the office and walked to the rapidly emptying parking lot.

Driving home Friday evening, the beginning of Memorial Day weekend, Nancie felt more discouraged than ever, although she had to admit Pete had a point. Alexa would hate him for sure.

She arrived at her apartment complex and parked her car. Then while she entered the building and collected her mail, she mentally listed friends she could phone and make plans with for the weekend. But after she'd placed several calls, she realized no one she knew was going to be available. They either had families or "significant others" to whom they were committed. And Wren had the girls. . .and Risa.

Once again, Nancie found herself totally alone.

eleven

"Hi, Ruth. Sorry to bother you. Any idea where Wren and the girls might be?"

Standing at her front door with a baby's arms wrapped around her knees, Ruth Baird smiled a greeting. "No bother. Come on in."

Nancie followed her into the house and decided that Ruth looked attractively disheveled tonight. Strands of her light brown hair had escaped their clip and fell loosely around her face. She wore a denim jumper over a red T-shirt, and on her feet were blue leather clogs.

"I suppose you have plans tonight," Nancie began once Ruth had guided her into the living room.

"No. Actually, I'm not sure what's going on. I'm waiting for Max to get home and tell me." She laughed. "We like to spend as much time as we can at the marina, but it looks like rain again, and I heard a news report say we're going to have bad weather all weekend."

"That figures."

Ruth sent her a sympathetic grin. "Hey, I just made a pot of flavored coffee. It's decaffeinated. Like a cup?"

"Sure."

Shooing her children into the basement playroom, Ruth made her way into the kitchen. She reappeared minutes later with two cups of steaming coffee that smelled distinctly of cinnamon.

"It's cinnamon hazelnut," Ruth affirmed.

"Thanks." Nancie took the proffered mug and brought it to her lips. "Mmm. . .delicious."

Smiling, Ruth sat down in the burgundy-upholstered

armchair. "You asked if I knew where Wren and the girls were, and I think I might. He picked them up at noon, since school let out early today, and mentioned planning to spend the weekend at a cabin up north. He said it was an annual thing."

"That's right. . . ." Nancie took another sip of her coffee, wondering how she could have forgotten. "Wren meets his brother up there. He's got two girls about the same ages as Alexa and Laura. And Steve is divorced, too, so both men have something in common. Two daughters and mean ex-wives."

"Oh, Nancie," Ruth stated, casting her a look of admonition, "I don't think you're mean." She took another swallow of coffee. "Is it imperative that you get ahold of Wren?"

"No. I just wanted to ask him if we could share the girls this weekend." She paused before adding, "My plans sort of fell through."

"What a shame."

Nancie shrugged.

"Well, Wren's plans almost came to an abrupt halt, too. He's had a chest cold that turned into bronchitis. From the way he was hacking, I was sure the poor guy had pneumonia. Finally, his station manager convinced him to see a doctor and he got some medicine."

Nancie raised an eyebrow. "Are you aware of who his station manager is?"

Ruth shook her head.

"Her name is Risa, and she's got designs on Wren. Big time."

"Really?"

Nancie nodded.

"Oh, boy. . ." Ruth's shapely brown brows furrowed with concern. "He said this week had been a real trial for him, and he asked me to keep him in prayer. Wren told me that his station manager had removed him from his route until he felt better and had put him in a position as her assistant. I just assumed he was struggling with the job change."

"He probably was."

"No, there was more to it. I realize that now. Wren's difficulties had to do with that woman. . . . What did you say her name is? Risa?"

Nancie nodded, but refused to probe further. She could only guess what had happened this week. Lucia had suddenly become the heroine in Wren's novel.

❧

"Women. Can't live with 'em, can't live without 'em."

"I'll say." Wren grinned at his brother's cliché, then proceeded to cough his fool head off.

"Man, are you sure you should be out here fishing in the rain with your cold?"

"No," Wren wheezed in reply, "I shouldn't be. And if I don't get better, Risa won't let me return to my route next week."

"So?"

"So, if I don't return to my route, I'll go crazy."

"Hmm. . .Risa's your boss?"

"Yep, but she wants to be something else."

"No kidding?" His brother raised curious brows.

"No kidding." Wren sighed and coughed again. "Steve," he confessed, "falling in love with her would be so easy."

"So what?"

"So. . .she's not a Christian, for one thing."

His older brother grunted out a disappointed reply, and Wren felt grateful that at least he understood that much, being a believer himself.

"Risa's got this way about her," he continued. "She makes me feel ten feet tall, she's caring, sweet, and she's a knockout. I've tried very hard not to notice her appearance, but she flaunts it, and she's starting to get to me."

"God doesn't tempt us beyond what we can bear. And He is faithful."

"I know, I know. . . ." Wren peered down at the lake, feeling as though he were drowning spiritually. "Nancie and I were getting along really well for a while. I had hoped we'd reconcile. But then I wrecked everything by kissing her one night. Alexa caught us, and Nancie hasn't spoken to me since."

Steve shot him a dubious glance. "Forget Nancie, will you? She did you a favor by divorcing you."

"I can't forget her. She's my daughters' mother." He paused, considering his brother through the hazy rain. "Can you forget Jean?"

"Yep."

Wren knew he'd come to their conversation's fork in the road, the point at which he and his brother no longer saw eye-to-eye. Steve harbored deep resentment against his ex-wife and Nancie, and he had no convictions about remarriage. It did no use to try and persuade him, either.

Wren was about to change the subject, when another coughing spell hit. "I think I'd better go back to the cabin and vegetate by the fire."

"Good idea. I'll vegetate with you so you won't have to swim to shore."

They shared a laugh.

≈

Nancie paced her bedroom, debating whether to drive up north and crash Wren's weekend at the cabin. He wouldn't care if she did, but Steve was likely to throttle her.

"Okay," she said, stopping in front of the telephone, "this will be my sign. If I call up there and anyone but Wren answers, I'll hang up and forget this whole idea."

Lifting the portable phone, she punched in the number from memory. She almost sighed with relief when she heard Wren's voice at the other end.

"Hi. It's Nancie, but don't let your brother know it's me!"

"Um. . .no, we didn't order any pizza."

Nancie grinned. "Quick thinking, Wren."

He rasped out a chuckle. "Not really. Nobody else is

around. Steve took all the girls roller skating in town and left me home so I can get rid of a cold."

"Ruth told me you were sick. Bronchitis, isn't it?"

"Yeah."

Nancie slowly lowered herself onto the edge of the bed. "Wren, I need a huge favor. I'm almost ashamed to even ask this of you, but. . ."

"But what?"

She swallowed down an odd sense of trepidation. Nancie hadn't ever been a coward. What was becoming of her? She shook her head. She needed to get some professional counseling.

But in the meantime, a couple of days up north might clear her head.

"Wren, as you know, I'm having a hard time with life in general," she began, "and I wondered if I could drive up and spend the weekend with you and the girls."

The long pause that met her question caused Nancie's heart to sink.

"Steve's up here with us," Wren finally said.

"I know."

Another pause.

"I don't think it's a good idea, Nancie."

"I realize I haven't given you much reason to want me around," she persisted, "but I promise I won't ruin your weekend. I'll be nice. I haven't forgotten how." She'd added the latter for a bit of levity, but didn't hear so much as a snicker issue from the receiver. "Please, Wren," she stated earnestly. "Please let me spend the weekend with you. There's plenty of room in the cabin, and I'll stay out of Steve's way." She momentarily fretted over her lower lip, then said, "Yours, too."

"I'm not worried about me. It's Steve. . . ." She heard him cover the receiver and cough for several long seconds. He didn't sound good. Not good at all.

"Wren, are you okay?"

He cleared his throat. "Yeah, I'll be fine."

"Well, look, I can help entertain the four girls if I come up, and that'll take some of the responsibility off your shoulders so you can rest. Tell Steve I'll cook and clean up the dishes so he won't have to lift a finger."

"You must be desperate," Wren quipped.

"I am," Nancie confessed in all seriousness. She expelled a heavy sigh. "I wish I could explain what I'm going through in a way that you'd understand, but I honestly don't know how to verbalize everything I'm feeling. I had even thought dating a guy at work would be a welcome distraction, but that never materialized—and it sure didn't help me sleep any better this past week."

"Have you seen a doctor?"

"That's my next step. But nothing's open this weekend."

"Wanna know what I think?"

"Hmm?" Nancie grimaced, sensing Wren was about to let her have it.

But to her amazement, he did no such thing.

"Nancie," he began in such a soft tone that it brought tears to her eyes, "I think you've been wound so tight for so long that you don't know how to relax anymore. Sure, come on up. But I honestly believe you need more rest than I do."

Her voice caught in her throat. "Thanks, Wren."

"You bet. What time should we expect you?"

"I can be there by noon tomorrow."

"See you then."

Nancie clicked off the portable phone, closed her eyes, and dropped her head back in relief. Wren was going to let her come to the cabin. *Maybe there is a God in heaven who loves me after all.*

twelve

Nancie thought the drive out of Milwaukee County and into Northern Wisconsin's wide-open spaces was therapy enough for her weary mind. Once she'd completed the four-and-a-half-hour road trip, she felt physically tired but emotionally uplifted from cruising through one pastoral scene after another.

Now all she needed was some sunshine on this gloomy day.

Opening the trunk of her car, Nancie pulled out her overnight bag and headed toward the cabin. She stopped abruptly, however, when her former brother-in-law blocked her entry.

"Hi, Steve," she said carefully. "Did Wren tell you I was coming?"

"Yeah, he told me. I'm not too happy about it, though."

He let the screen door slam shut behind him and stepped forward. Nancie squared her shoulders, anticipating trouble.

"But as long as you're here, I'm going to tell you just what I think of you." Steve wagged an accusatory finger at her. "You're a bloodsucker. You suck the life out of people in order to get what you want, and then you dump them by the wayside. You don't care who you hurt as long as you get your way. You're no good, Nancie."

She opened her mouth to hurl back a retort, but closed it again, remembering her promise to Wren. She'd have to buck up and take the insults. . .this time.

"I suppose you're sorry you didn't get this place from Wren when you took him to the cleaners for everything else!"

Nancie didn't reply, but slowly set down her bag on the pavement.

"Well, I made sure you couldn't touch it." Steve raised his voice. "This cabin has been in our family for generations."

"I never wanted the cabin," she told him tersely.

"Good. Because you won't get your hooks into this property like you did the house in Shorewood. You sold that one right out from under my brother and didn't give a whit about him or the girls."

"Steve, that's enough," Wren called through the door. The next instant, he was outside on the walkway, standing between her and his brother.

"Whatever problems you've got right now, Nancie," Steve shouted around Wren, "you deserve 'em. Every last one."

The barb met its mark and she winced, although she somehow managed to hold her tongue and keep her word to Wren. But, oh, how she itched to put Steve in his place! She had enough dirt on him to do her own share of mudslinging. And he called himself a Christian? Right. That's not what she'd heard from his ex-wife.

"And another thing," Steve began. However, before he could get another word formed, Wren grabbed hold of the front of his green sweatshirt and brought him up short.

"I said that's enough," he told his brother, a muscle working in his jaw.

Steve glared at him, then pushed him away, and stalked back into the cabin.

After watching him go, Wren turned to Nancie with a look of apology. "That wasn't supposed to happen. Steve and I talked about this last night."

"Don't worry about it," she said flatly. "He obviously had some venting to do." Whether from containing her anger all this time or feeling wounded after the verbal assault, tears pooled in Nancie's eyes. She blinked and glanced away so Wren wouldn't see her cry. "I guess I shouldn't have come."

"Well, you're here now, so let's make the most of it." Wren coughed hard before stooping to pick up her bag. "Steve won't bother you again."

She nodded subtly and looked on as Wren disappeared into the cabin. She didn't follow him. She couldn't. Not yet. She needed to regain her composure.

Turning, she surveyed the landscape. Not much had changed since she'd been here last. Towering pine trees still loomed overhead, while beyond them the grassy knoll grew lush and green from all the rain. And the same dirt path wound its way down the hill to the lake.

The screen door slammed and Nancie assumed it was Wren. But then she heard the soft, questioning voice come from behind her.

"Aunt Nancie?"

She swung around and peered at her niece, who stared back at her curiously. Nancie decided the girl resembled the Nickelsons with her dark brown hair and dark eyes, and she looked as though she could be Alexa's sister.

"Heather." Nancie smiled warmly. "My goodness, you're so grown up."

"I'm thirteen now."

"You look sixteen."

The girl beamed, obviously pleased by the comment. But then her smile faded. "Don't mind my dad," she said in a hushed tone. "He yells all the time."

Before Nancie could reply, the door banged again and Alexa stepped out of the house.

"Hi," Nancie said, unsure of what her daughter's reaction might be. Would it mirror Steve's?

Much to her surprise, Alexa closed the distance between them and slipped her arms around Nancie's waist. "Hi, Mom," she said, laying her head on Nancie's shoulder. "Uncle Steve shouldn't have said those mean things to you."

Nancie sucked in a breath. It was the first display of affection Nancie had received from her oldest daughter in a long, long while. Reveling in it, she stroked Alexa's hair and kissed the top of her head. "Thanks, sweetie."

"Hey, Lex, maybe your mom will take us to see that movie!"

Alexa pulled back and gazed up into Nancie's face. "Will you?"

"What movie are we talking about?"

The two girls immediately began to chatter about the story line and the actor in the leading role. Obviously he was the latest teenage heartthrob.

Alexa still had her arms around Nancie, so she could hardly refuse the request. Besides, it gave her the purpose for coming up here that she'd so desperately needed. "Sure, I'd be happy to take you guys to a movie."

"And maybe we could go shopping, too," Heather added.

"Dad and Uncle Steve hate shopping. Besides, Dad's sick."

"Oh, you poor girls," Nancie crooned jokingly. "You've suffered such hardships."

Alexa smirked.

"Well, let's go find out when the movie starts and plan our afternoon."

"Mandi and Laura will have to tag along," Heather said as they strolled to the cabin.

"That's all right." With her arms around both girls' shoulders, Nancie ushered them inside.

She walked up the few steps from the mudroom, deciding this place hadn't changed; and it smelled just as musty as she remembered. One great room had long ago been divided into a kitchen and living room, marked off by the sink and wooden cupboards arranged in a half-wall design on one side and more cabinets on the other. This allowed someone cooking or washing dishes to see everything that was going on at the other end of the dwelling. Doorways leading into the three bedrooms and one bathroom were accessible to the left, and to the right, a large addition ran the entire length of the cabin—it included a sunporch on the living-room side and a spacious dining area off the kitchen.

"Aunt Nancie is taking us into town," Heather blurted.

Standing close together near the fireplace, Wren and Steve ceased their conversation at once. Nancie could only guess what—make that whom—they were discussing.

In that moment, she realized Steve's hostility wouldn't have fazed her a month ago. But combined with the mugging incident, the gossip at work, Risa's remarks, and her own depressed mood, his animosity seemed to suddenly crush her into a hopeless mass.

"Can we go, Dad?" Alexa asked Wren.

He glanced Nancie's way and smiled, although it looked forced. "Sure. It's fine by me." He looked back at his brother. "What do you think, Steve?"

"I'm for anything that'll get *her* out of here."

"Sweet!" Heather cried excitedly. She seemed oblivious to her father's insult of Nancie. "C'mon, Lex. Let's get ready." The two older girls dashed off into one of the bedrooms with the younger ones in tow.

"Steve. . ." Wren frowned a warning at his brother.

"I can't help it." With that, he stomped out onto the sunporch.

Wren turned to Nancie again and gave her a rueful shrug. "Again, I'm sorry." He lowered himself into a nearby armchair. Placing his elbows on his knees, he rubbed his hands over his face in a weary gesture before lifting his gaze to hers once more. "I had really hoped to avoid any confrontations. Last night Steve told me he disliked the idea of your visit, but he didn't object to it. I would have phoned you and told you not to come if I'd known how he would be."

"Sounds to me like Steve had a good twelve hours to gear up so he could blast me when I arrived."

"I suppose so. . . ." Wren shook his head. "But I do appreciate the way you didn't blast him back."

Nancie narrowed her gaze. "I wanted to, believe me."

He grinned. "I'm sure. And I'm amazed at your self-control."

She lifted her shoulders, feigning indifference. "I promised I'd be nice and it was never my intention to ruin anyone's weekend, although it seems I've done exactly that just by showing up."

Wren scratched his jaw thoughtfully with his left hand, and Nancie noticed he'd taken off his wedding ring. She stared at his bare finger, wondering what to make of it. However, before she could ask, the girls swarmed her.

"Can I sit in the front seat on the way there?" Heather asked.

"Can we buy ice cream?" her younger sister followed up.

Laura tugged on the hem of Nancie's oversized shirt. "Can I sit in the front seat on the way home?"

"Are we going shopping first?" Alexa wanted to know.

"Have fun," Wren called over the din, looking amused.

"Oh, we will," Nancie replied. "This beats sitting home alone any day. But can I borrow your car? I don't have enough seat belts in mine."

Wren nodded and pulled the keys out of his pants pocket. Alexa snatched them and ran outside, declaring that she was going to start up her dad's vehicle. The other children darted after her.

Nancie tossed her keys to Wren. "Feel free to use my car while I'm gone if you need to." On that note, Nancie exited the cabin and joined the girls.

ॐ

So far, so good, Wren thought as he reclined comfortably in the corner of the living room. He covered himself with a thick blanket and basked in the heat radiating from the blazing fireplace. A fever he could live with; contention between his brother and ex-wife, he couldn't. But in the time since Nancie had returned with the girls, bearing two large pizzas as peace offerings, no arguments had erupted.

Steve suddenly entered the kitchen, dumped his plate in

the sink, and walked toward him, chewing the last of his crusty supper. "Okay, maybe she is trying to be nice," he whispered. "My question is, why? What does she want?"

"Nothing. It's like I said. She's burned out from school and work and she needs to relax. This is a great place to do exactly that, don't you think?"

A dubious expression crossed his face. "I don't know. . . ."

"Did you apologize for going ballistic earlier?"

"Nope, and I don't intend to, either."

"Steve, I thought we agreed. Your Christian testimony is at stake here. How's Nancie ever going to come to know the Lord if she doesn't see Him in us?"

"If she hasn't been converted by now, she never will be."

"You don't know that!"

Just then Nancie walked into the kitchen and cast a wary glance their way. "Are you feeling any better, Wren?"

"Like she really cares," Steve retorted under his breath.

Wren widened his gaze beseechingly before looking toward the sink, which Nancie had begun to fill with soap and water. "I'm fine," he replied.

One by one, the girls brought in their supper dishes. Before washing them, Nancie wiped down the dining table so the four cousins could play a board game. When she returned to the sink and stuck her hands in the bubbly water, Steve set down the newspaper he'd been reading and sauntered over to her side. Wren rose slowly, praying that his brother would mind his manners.

He didn't. He tore into Nancie shamelessly. Wren wanted to intervene, but he couldn't seem to muster the energy to referee. He felt like a feeble observer.

After Steve had had his say, Nancie opened her mouth to have hers. . .and Wren held his breath. This was going to get ugly. He knew his ex-wife was capable of shredding a guy, and he ought to know, having been the recipient of many a vicious tongue-lashing. While Steve might deserve it, Wren didn't think he could watch. His brother had no idea what he was in for.

And he certainly didn't want the kids to overhear!

Quickly making his way to the other end of the kitchen, Wren closed the double doors to the dining area. Pivoting, he leaned against them. To his astonishment, Nancie had gone back to washing dishes without uttering a syllable. Her blond hair partially covered her face, but Wren still saw the tears slipping down her cheeks as she kept her gaze fastened to the soapsuds. His heart went out to her.

He looked over at his brother then and suddenly felt like knocking his block off!

Steve met his stare. "Even when we were teens, you always fell for the bad girls."

"Will you quit already?!"

"Nope. I'm not done yet. I've figured out what she's up to. Nancie's no fool, and she knows how much you'd like to get your family back together. So she's playing with you, Wren. That's right. She's up here for the sole purpose of destroying your chance at happiness with that woman you're in love with. . .Risa."

Wren's heart just about leapt into his throat. His brother had no right to divulge such information—and it wasn't even true. Sure he had feelings for Risa, feelings he wasn't about to deny. But he wasn't certain they could be labeled "love." Besides, he had yet to earnestly seek God's face in the matter.

Nevertheless, he gauged Nancie's reaction. He'd suspected that she was jealous of his relationship with Risa. But would she really go to such lengths to keep them apart?

Nancie shook the soap off her hands, wiped away her errant tears, then grabbed the dish towel. Facing Wren, she tipped her head. "Well, now I know why you suddenly removed your wedding band."

"See, I told you!" Steve exclaimed, giving Wren's shoulder a shove.

"You wanna get lost for a while?" he replied irritably.

"Sure. I'll go play that Barbie board game with the girls." Looking smug, Steve left them alone.

Wren resumed his inquisitive regard of Nancie while she fidgeted with the dish towel. At last, she set it down.

"Look, Wren," she said in a straightforward manner, "I'm not going to stand in the way of your newfound happiness with Risa. Okay, so I'm envious. Fine. I'll admit it. But I'm hardly the villain your brother described."

Tapering his gaze, Wren inched his way forward. "I'm just curious. Who are you envious of—Risa. . .or me?"

"What?" Nancie frowned, obviously confused.

"Well, if you're envious of me, then I'd say it's because you've been looking for Mr. Right and haven't found him. But if you're envious of Risa, then I'd be inclined to wonder if maybe somewhere in the back of your mind you're harboring hopes of reconciliation."

Nancie smiled, and it was the first time Wren had seen her look even remotely cheerful all day. "I think I'll plead the Fifth on that one," she said, folding her arms in front of her. She looked more like the Nancie he knew. . .and, yes, loved.

"If you don't answer my question," Wren persisted, trying to conceal a grin, "I'll be forced to draw my own conclusions."

"All right, I'll answer it. But I'll have to think about it first." Her smile faded. "I honestly don't know what I'm feeling these days, Wren. My life is in a tangled knot that I'm trying desperately to untie. Before it's too late."

"What does that mean, 'before it's too late'?"

"I don't know," she whispered, turning back to the sinkful of dishes. "That's what frightens me. I just don't know."

thirteen

Wren sipped his coffee as he stood at the picture window in the dining area; he was watching Nancie, who was down by the lake. He knew she hadn't slept much last night, because he hadn't, either. Between his coughing fits and her insomnia, they'd ended up sitting in the living room together. Then he'd pulled out the medical thriller he was reading. It had been written by a Christian couple, and as usual, Wren quickly became absorbed in the plot. Nancie soon asked if he had something she could read, so he'd directed her to a shelf of inspirational romances—called Heartsong Presents—that were published by a Christian company. He explained that his mother had grown fond of the sleek little novels. Nancie elected to give one a try, and before either of them knew it, dawn had brightened the eastern sky.

"Hey, what are you looking at out there?" Steve peered over his shoulder and groaned loudly. "Oh. It's *her*."

"And 'her' is making me very nervous."

"How come?"

Wren glanced at his brother. "Nancie can't swim and it looks like she's standing on the very edge of the dock."

He set down his mug, unable to stand there another moment worrying about her. Without a word to Steve, he made for the door and headed down the winding path, trying to make some noise as he went so he wouldn't startle her. He even coughed for several long moments before reaching the water.

"Hey, Nancie," he called, stepping out on the dock. He paused by one of the large wooden supports. "Looks like the sky is clearing."

When she didn't respond, he moved closer.

"Whatcha doing?"

"Thinking," she finally replied, her gaze lingering on the murky water.

"Well. . ." Wren grabbed hold of her waist and pulled her back several feet. "I'd prefer that you do your thinking away from the edge of the dock, thank you very much."

She turned and looked up at him as a slow smile spread across her face. "Wren, the most incredible thing just happened."

He raised his brows expectantly.

"It started earlier this morning. I was remembering everything your brother said, and it really upset me. Mostly because I realized a lot of it is true." Nancie faced the lake again, folding her arms over her thick, multicolored cotton sweater. "I came down here feeling utterly hopeless, believing I was unlovable. And like Steve said, I deserved it. I felt like it wouldn't have mattered if I lived or died."

"Nancie. . ."

"I actually contemplated suicide, Wren," she continued. "I don't know if I would have gone that far, but I shudder to think that the idea even crossed my mind."

A tiny grin curved her lips. "But then this slim ray of sunshine broke through the clouds. It was there and then gone again in a matter of moments, but I saw it." Closing her eyes briefly, she shook her head. "Wren, I know that was God. He showed me something similar on Friday night, too. That shaft of light was another sign from Him, letting me know He really exists."

The nervous swell in Wren's chest began to subside. He'd been ready to check Nancie into the nearest hospital, but suddenly he got the feeling that wouldn't be necessary.

Her grin broadened. "I got that much settled anyway. There's really a God up there, just like you've been telling me for years. But, unfortunately, the realization didn't make my depression magically vanish, so I asked Him if anybody on earth still cared about me." She paused and laughed before pushing her windblown blond hair out of her face. "And then you came coughing your way down from the cabin." Her eyes grew misty, but she blinked away the tears and gazed off in the distance.

"You know I care about you, Nancie. I've never stopped caring about you."

"I know." She sounded contrite.

"And Alexa and Laura love you."

"I know that, too. I'm a very fortunate woman."

"Yes, you are."

"But I've taken a lot of things—a lot of people—for granted, haven't I?"

"Ah, well, I guess I can't argue with you there."

She peered at him from beneath an arched brow and smiled. Tipping her head to one side, she considered him with longing in her eyes that Wren hadn't seen in years.

"Will you kiss me?" she asked almost meekly.

The request took him by surprise; however, he was more than happy to oblige.

Stepping forward, he slipped his arms around her waist and pulled her to him. Then he slowly lowered his mouth to hers, drinking in its softness. They shared a breath and something more—something akin to the oneness Wren had never experienced with any other woman, or ever would. He knew that now. They were made for each other.

Drawing his head back, Wren searched her face. Her eyelids fluttered open and she regarded him dreamily.

"I forgot what a good kisser you are," she murmured, her arms still wrapped around his neck.

"You're not so bad yourself."

"Kind of out of practice."

Wren smiled. "Glad to hear it."

She gave him a look of chagrin.

Suddenly a bronchospasm erupted, extinguishing the heat of the moment.

"Sorry, Nancie," he sputtered. "I totally forgot I was sick when I kissed you."

"I totally forgot myself." She laughed softly. "Oh, well, too late to worry about that now," she said, looping her arm around his elbow. "But maybe we'd better get you back inside the cabin. This damp air can't be good for you."

Wren allowed her to lead him up the path. He thought things seemed so perfect between them now—just like when, years ago, their marriage had been sailing on smoothly and they'd loved each other with an unbridled passion and stead-fast devotion. But then a wedge had come between them—a wedge that existed to this day and always would, unless Nancie came to Christ.

But Wren sensed she was close. So close. . .

　　　　　　　　　　🙠

Nancie decided to accompany Wren, Steve, and the girls to church. The message was one she'd heard before—nothing new. Over the years she'd gone to church with Wren quite often, especially after his conversion experience, but then she'd enrolled in school and had better things to do on Sunday morning. And once the service ended this morning, she had to admit that the idea of biblical Christianity being the only right and true religion irked her just as much as it ever had. Oh, she might have changed her view of God—He existed and there was a heaven—but wasn't He the same God the Buddhists and other religions prayed to? As long as a person believed in God, wasn't that enough?

She verbalized her opinions to Wren on the way back to the cabin. But it was Alexa who spoke up.

"The devil believes in God and Jesus, too, Mom," she said from the backseat. "But he's not going to be in heaven."

Sitting in the driver's seat of Nancie's car, Wren glanced at his daughter in the rearview mirror and grinned. "That's right, Lex."

"The devil believes?" Nancie shook her head. "Okay, now

I'm totally confused. But forget it. I don't want to talk about this anymore. Let's change the subject."

Turning her head, she watched the scenery whiz by as they rode through town.

Finally Wren drove up the gravel road, and Steve's vehicle came into view. Obviously he and his girls had beaten them home. Nancie crawled out of the passenger side of the car, and Wren tossed her the keys over the roof.

"It's a fun little car to drive," he said, "but it's definitely too small for me."

"It's perfect for me in the city. I can find a parking space almost anywhere."

"I believe it."

Alexa and Laura led the way into the cabin. Their cousins were in the process of changing from their Sunday dresses into play clothes. In the kitchen, Steve had set a package of ground beef on the counter.

"I thought we'd barbecue this afternoon," he said, emerging from one of the bedrooms in shorts and a T-shirt. "It turned out to be a pretty nice day."

Nancie nodded, thinking that was about the only thing she and her former brother-in-law agreed on—the weather.

In the room she shared with Alexa and Heather, Nancie changed her clothes, too, pulling on jeans and a cranberry-colored, short-sleeved cotton blouse. When she finished, she realized the cabin was silent. Peering out the dining-area window, she saw that everyone else was down at the lake. Steve and Wren were in the boat, starting the engine. All six wore fluorescent orange life jackets. She watched, but didn't feel left out at all. Boat rides had never been her idea of a good time. She had always preferred dry land.

Leaving the window, she made another pot of coffee in the kitchen. It didn't feel all that warm outside to her. The sun shone brightly, but the temperature felt all of seventy-five degrees. Once she'd filled a mug with the steaming brew, she traipsed down the pathway to the lake, intending to sit on the dock and observe the activities from there. Much to her delight and surprise, Heather was up on the water skis—shorts, T-shirt, life jacket, and all—while her father manned the motorboat and her cousins cheered her on.

In no time, other boats were on the small lake, whirring noisily past the dock. Nancie watched as Alexa tried to water-ski, but each time she stood, she fell into the water. Even so, Nancie enjoyed the spectacle without a single worry. Unlike herself, her daughters had learned to swim at an early age.

While Wren pulled Alexa into the boat, Nancie let her gaze wander to the other side of the lake. She spied a small row-boat gliding across the water, doing its best to stay out of the way of the more powerful, motorized crafts. As she looked on, she saw the man with the oars row and row, while a tow-headed toddler—a little boy, perhaps—stood atop one of the benches, pointing to something on the shore.

That kid is going to fall in, Nancie thought, wishing the adult would make the baby sit down. And no life jacket? Nancie shook her head in dismay.

Just then, exactly as she predicted, the child toppled over-board. She stood up and jogged to the end of the dock, thinking she would soon see the man dive in after him, but all he did was stand up in his rowboat and begin calling for help.

What an idiot! She cupped her hands and hollered to Wren and Steve. After gaining their attention, she pointed across the lake. Steve revved the motor, and the entire crew was there in no time. Seconds later, Wren and Steve both dove into the lake while Nancie stood and watched in horror.

Suddenly Nancie realized this wasn't just a little accident anymore, it was a full-blown emergency. Racing to the cabin, she grabbed her cell phone and called 911. She gave the operator the appropriate information, and then, her phone still in hand, she returned to the dock. She got there just in time to see Steve handing the man in the rowboat the child's lifeless form. Unfortunately, the guy didn't know what to do next, so Steve catapulted himself over the side of the boat and attempted to resuscitate the boy.

Finally the rescue squad appeared and stood beside Nancie on the dock. All three called to Wren. "Bring the child here! Bring the child here!"

In a flash, Steve handed over the little one, from rowboat to motor boat, and Wren sped across the water. As the paramedics labored over the little boy right there on the dock, Nancie helped the girls out of the boat. All four wore anxious expressions, yet none of them had panicked during the ordeal, and Nancie marveled at their courage. She herself was quaking inside.

Once the child was immobilized and intubated, he was carried to the awaiting ambulance and rushed to the hospital.

"I hope he makes it," Nancie said in a shaky voice.

Wren shook his head sadly. "I'm afraid he's already dead."

"But those emergency technicians, they—"

"Nancie, they have to do all that. Now it's up to the doctors at the hospital. And yeah, by some miracle, I hope he makes it, too. But Steve couldn't get him breathing."

Tears started streaming down Heather's small face. Soon they all wept, and Nancie gathered as many girls in her arms as she could hold. Across the lake, Steve was assisting the man in the rowboat to shore.

"Is that the child's father?" Nancie asked in between sobs.

Wren shook his head. "It's his uncle or cousin or something. I'm not quite sure. Apparently he was baby-sitting."

"Oh, no. . ." Nancie's heart seemed to plunge to her toes, and her tears flowed all the harder. Wren put a comforting arm around her, and she buried her face in his shoulder. "S–somewhere," she stuttered sorrowfully, "there's a mother out there who has no idea she just lost her precious little boy forever."

fourteen

The afternoon had passed in a repressed silence, a conse-quence of the tragedy on the lake only hours earlier. Wren, Steve, and the girls had said prayers for the child, and Nancie had added her own silent plea. But at around suppertime the police arrived, asking questions for their report. They divulged the news that the little boy, whose name was Nathan, had indeed died at the hospital.

"Man, if we'd only found him in time," Steve muttered after the police had gone and they all sat around the dining table. "But that lake was so dark and murky from all the rain, I couldn't see my hand in front of my face underwater, let alone a drowning kid."

"You did what you could, Steve," Nancie told him. "Don't torture yourself."

He shook his head in sad reply, then sipped his coffee.

"The water was so cold," Alexa added, "that it took my breath away when I first jumped in to try waterskiing. That's probably what happened to little Nathan. He probably gulped water right into his lungs and sank to the bottom."

"Oh, man, if we'd just found him sooner," Steve murmured again.

Nancie exchanged concerned glances with Wren.

"Steve, that boy died despite our efforts," Wren stated emphatically, "not because of them. Let it go."

"Yeah, Uncle Steve," Laura said with a caring note in her sweet voice, "we can at least be happy that Nathan is in heaven with Jesus right now."

A hint of a grin tugged at the corners of Steve's mouth.

Nancie cleared her throat. "Laura, honey, we don't know if

little Nathan is in heaven." She peered over her youngest's blond head at the two men. "Come on, guys, let's not heap deception onto our grief. I mean, we don't know what kind of family Nathan had. What if his parents don't even believe in God?"

"Nancie, salvation is a decision," Steve informed her as he gazed into his mug. "Doesn't matter what someone's parents believe. A person has to be able to understand what sin is, realize his need for the Savior, and then make the decision to get saved. Babies can't do that. . .that's what God's grace is for."

Wren agreed. "I think of King David in the Bible, when he was mourning the death of his infant son—the one Bathsheba gave him. He said something like, 'I will go to him, but he won't return to me.' The implication is that David knew he'd see the baby in heaven someday."

"See, Aunt Nancie?" Heather said. "Little Nathan's in heaven."

"That's quite the Bible lesson," she replied sarcastically. But, noting all the responsive faces staring at her, she knew she was outnumbered in this debate.

Changing the subject altogether, she glanced at her wristwatch. "It's almost seven. I think we should all eat something." She stood, suddenly thunderstruck. "Good grief, I sound like my mother." Looking over at Wren and Steve, she added, "I sound like *your* mother!"

Wren hooted before lapsing into one of his coughing fits, and for the first time in hours, Steve cracked a full-fledged smile.

≈

Wren sneezed and pulled the thick blanket around him before moving the recliner closer to the fire. His body ached from the hair follicles on his head to his toenails. "I think that swim in the lake this afternoon did me in," he told his brother, who sat across the room on the couch.

"I'll bet it did."

A girlish shrill wafted in from the sunporch, and Steve glanced in that direction.

"Sounds like they're having fun," Wren remarked, situating himself in the chair before bringing his feet up. He sighed. Much better. Now if only that cold medicine would kick in.

"Our daughters were discussing hairstyles and makeup, last I heard."

Wren smiled. "See? It's a good thing Nancie came up this weekend. She's kept all four girls busy since supper."

Steve sat forward. "As long as you brought up the subject. . ."

Wren groaned. "Don't start, Steve."

He ignored the request. "Listen, I saw you and Nancie out on the dock this morning. I had to keep the kids away from the window, 'cause I couldn't decide if it was PG-13 or not."

Wren closed his eyes. "I kissed my ex-wife. Big deal."

"It was the way you kissed her that I'm talking about. You're going to get hurt all over again. May I remind you that I'm the guy whose shoulder you cried on after Nancie threw you out of the house and said she didn't love you anymore?"

Wren opened his eyes and saw his brother toss a thumb toward the porch.

"That's the same woman."

"People change."

"Not her. She's got an agenda, and she's using you to accomplish whatever it is she wants now."

"That's not true. Nancie's burned out, and I honestly think God is working through these circumstances to reach her heart. In fact, I have an inkling Nancie wants to reconcile. After all, she knows how I feel about her and she's done nothing but encourage me this weekend."

"It's a game with her, Wren."

He shook his head. No. This time it was for real. . .for keeps.

"Whatever." Steve held a section of the newspaper over his face. The conversation had ended.

Feeling drowsy, Wren closed his eyes and slept.

Sometime later, he awoke to find Nancie sitting where Steve had been. She was eyeing him speculatively, so Wren sat up a little straighter.

"What are you staring at? Was I drooling?" He wiped his mouth and chin self-consciously.

"No, you weren't drooling," she replied with a soft laugh. "I was just watching you sleep and thinking about everything that happened today—mostly your heroics in trying to save little Nathan." Holding up the novel in her hand, she added, "I must be enjoying these romances too much."

Grinning, Wren resumed his comfy position on the recliner. His eyelids felt heavy, so he closed them.

"Have you ever thought seriously about writing a book?"

"Sure I have. I think anyone who enjoys writing dreams of authoring a best-seller."

"Will yours be a romance?"

He couldn't help smiling as he thought about his characters. Pretty soon George and Nan would discover the hidden treasure within the castle walls. Then Lucia was going to show up and wreak havoc between them.

"I guess I like more of a mystery," he finally replied. "But the romance will be part of the plot because that's what sells. . .or so I've been told."

"You're going to try and sell your book?"

Wren peered at Nancie through one eye. She sounded alarmed for some odd reason. "Well, if I ever get a whole book written, I might submit it to a publisher. But I'm an amateur. Right now I write for fun, and that's it."

"Oh. Well, that's good."

Wren closed his eyes again.

"If you ever need any help writing the romance angle, feel free to ask me."

Both eyes snapped opened and regarded her this time.

Nancie's soft brown eyes twinkled mischievously before

she resumed her reading.

Wren thought up a reply, but coughed instead of speaking, then moaned as the pain in his chest spread like fire.

"You're not feeling any better, are you?"

"Oh, I'll be fine."

"Sure you will."

"What about you?" he countered. "Aren't you going to try to get some sleep?"

"Yes, but I'm waiting for Alexa and Heather to quit chatting before I go to bed. I'm all talked out for one day." Nancie sighed. "Those girls never run out of things to say!"

Wren smiled before drifting off to sleep once again.

&

Memorial Day dawned bright and sunny. Steve took Nancie and the girls to a parade in town while Wren continued his convalescence at the cabin. All seemed well, until they returned around noon. Nancie looked upset, and Steve was furious. Wren didn't even have to ask what had happened. He knew.

"The wicked witch of the west pales in comparison to your ex-wife," Steve said, poking his index finger into Wren's chest.

"Now what did you do?"

"Me?"

From over Steve's shoulder, Wren saw Nancie carrying out her overnight bag. Shouldering his brother out of his way, he started after her.

"Let her go," Steve said, catching his arm. "She doesn't love you. I asked her point-blank. She's using you, just as I thought."

"Aw, Steve," Wren moaned, "why couldn't you have minded your own business?"

"Because you're my brother and I don't want you to get hurt again." Steve gave him a pitiful look. "Fine. Don't believe me. Go ask her. Hear it for yourself."

Wren strode purposely from the cabin, half wishing

Nancie would drive off before they could talk. *Lord, help me handle the truth,* he prayed, *whatever it is.*

Nancie was standing near her car, telling the girls good-bye, when he reached her.

"Hey, let's go fishing one last time before we head home," Steve called, and the kids went running off in the direction of the lake, squealing merrily. Wren felt grateful to his brother for coming up with the quick diversion, although it might not have been necessary had Steve kept his mouth shut.

"Nancie?"

She refused to look at him at first, and Wren wasn't sure how to begin the conversation, so they stood on the gravel drive in strained silence for what seemed like a millennium.

Finally, she whirled around angrily. "He pushed my buttons, Wren, and I lost it. I couldn't help it. I tried to put up and shut up all weekend, but your brother crossed the line this morning."

"Were the girls around?"

"No. They were in the stands, watching the parade. I was on my way back from the concession stand when Steve cornered me. He insulted me again and I threw my lemonade in his face. Then I told him off."

"Oh, boy. . ." Wren looked heavenward. He could well imagine the scene.

"Want to hear more?"

"No." He scratched his jaw thoughtfully, then dropped his hand to his side. "But. . .Steve told me you said some things. Things about you and me. Would you mind repeating them?"

Leaning up against her car, Nancie stared straight ahead into the woods. Her arms were folded tightly over her light blue, long-sleeved T-shirt. With her blond hair pulled back into a loose ponytail, she made a fetching sight in spite of the circumstances.

"Nancie, will you tell me? Please?"

A muscle worked in her cheek before she answered. "He

pushed me to my limit, Wren."

"Okay. So you lost your temper. What did you say? Did you mean it?"

She turned and faced him, lifting an obstinate chin. "Yeah, I guess I meant it. I said it. I said I didn't love you. You've heard that before, right?" She produced a curt laugh. "Steve also accused me of using you this weekend, and maybe I did. I was hurting and I needed someone. I knew you'd be there for me, so. . . ." She swallowed hard. "So I used you. Fine. I admit it."

Gazing deeply into her amber eyes, Wren didn't believe a word of it. Oh, she might have said those things in the heat of a rage, but she hadn't meant them. At the moment, she looked as sorry as a little girl who was about to lose her best friend.

"Well, Nancie," he replied at last, "if you used me, I can't say I didn't enjoy every minute of it."

She blinked incredulously, and Wren almost laughed out loud at her expression.

She shook her head as if to clear it. "You should hate me. Scream. Yell. Call me every rotten name you can think of."

"And what would that prove? That I'm no better than my brother? No, I think not. Steve's a bitter man. He's got so much animosity inside him stemming from his own divorce that I've actually begun to worry about him."

Nancie's features softened, but she still seemed perplexed by his composure.

He looked at his wristwatch. "I'm probably going to leave here in a couple of hours, or whenever the girls are done fishing," he said, changing the subject. "Will you be home if I drop Laura off later this evening?"

She nodded, then opened her car door. "Thanks, Wren," she murmured before scooting in behind the wheel.

Within minutes, she accelerated down the road.

He whispered a prayer as he watched her go. "Lord, thank You for Your infinite grace. I'd be a leveled man right now without it."

fifteen

All day Tuesday, Nancie tried to concentrate on her work at the office, but her efforts were in vain. She couldn't stop thinking of Wren and the way he had stood there calmly when she'd said she didn't love him. He hadn't even flinched. Of course, she'd told him that a hundred times if she'd told him once.

Except this time, it just wasn't true.

In her heart of hearts, Nancie acknowledged that something had happened to her over the weekend—something indefinable yet life-changing. Her very thought process wasn't the same. Suddenly her views on God, family, and death were very different. She now realized that the realm of humanism was flanked by an isolation she couldn't tolerate. In tailoring herself for the world of success, her values had gotten skewed. Now she had to reprioritize and reclaim what was once hers.

But did she really want to? And was it too late?

Perhaps.

Steve had said Wren was in love with Risa. Nancie decided it might be true, and she wondered if the fiery redhead was the reason why Wren hadn't buckled under her false admission yesterday afternoon. At the same time, she couldn't be sure. The way Wren had kissed her Sunday morning communicated quite the opposite. Did he kiss Risa the same way?

Nancie expelled a wondering sigh.

And then there was the memory of Nathan's drowning fresh in her mind. She had contemplated dying that same day and in the same way. But ironically, it was a small child who'd lost his life in the lake, not her.

Life was so fragile, Nancie realized, and she felt as though hers lay in pieces. A broken marriage, broken relationships. . . and her children were products of a broken home. It was all her doing, and now she could add a broken heart to the list.

~

When Wren saw the showers early Tuesday morning, he knew Risa would never let him walk his mail route. He also realized he couldn't work alongside her inside the station again. He didn't think he felt strong enough to work, period, so he decided to do something he'd never done in all his years at the post office. . . . He called in sick.

Next he made another appointment with his doctor, who gave him a stronger antibiotic and cough syrup, in addition to a work excuse for the rest of the week. Wren protested. One day off was all he needed. But after the physician threatened hospitalization, explaining that Wren was on the brink of developing pneumonia, he promised to comply.

Once back home, Wren gave himself permission to be totally lazy. Sprawled on the couch, he watched television. Soon his mind wandered, and he thought about Risa. He thought about Nancie. One woman said she loved him, the other said she didn't. Unfortunately, the one who didn't was the one he still dreamed about at night, and just thinking of the triangular mess caused an empty pang in Wren's heart. He needed someone to love him and, likewise, he longed for someone to love. Was he wasting his time pining for Nancie and a reconciliation that would never be?

Suddenly Wren curtailed his wayward thoughts. He had no business considering a romantic relationship with either woman. They didn't share his faith.

Forgive me, Lord. You know what I want, what I need. Help me to wait patiently for You to give it to me.

~

Risa felt so bad when she heard Wren was even more ill than he'd been the previous week, that she phoned her Nana

Mandelini and asked her to cook up a batch of her famous chicken noodle soup.

"Are you sick?" came the worried reply with a hint of an accent from the "old country."

"No, no. The soup's for a friend. He's got a bad case of bronchitis."

"He? Tell me about this 'he.' "

Risa grinned. Her grandmother had been trying to marry her off since she was sixteen. "Oh, there's not much to tell yet."

"I hope he's Italian."

"Ah. . .no, he's not."

A pause. "Well maybe I'll like him anyhow."

Risa laughed softly. "You'll like him a lot, if you ever get to meet him. He's polite and kind and goes to church, but he's. . .well. . .we're just friends right now."

The older woman muttered something in Italian that Risa interpreted to mean, "A man and a woman can never be just friends."

She grinned. That's what she was counting on!

"Can you make the soup, Nana?"

"Yah, yah, I'll maka the soup."

"Great. I'll pick it up after work—about five-thirty. Is that okay?"

"Yah, okay."

Risa gave her grandmother a smooch through the phone line. "You're the best, Nana. Ciao."

❧

"What do you mean, Wren called in sick?" Nancie couldn't believe what Ruth was telling her. "He's never called in sick. He must be dying!"

Ruth lifted her hands helplessly. "He phoned me this morning and said he'd drive Alexa to school, but asked if I'd pick her up since he didn't know when he'd get an appointment at the clinic. That's when he told me he'd called into work, and I haven't heard from him since."

Nancie glanced at her watch. She'd worked late this evening in an effort to make up for her daydreaming, and now it was after six. She looked at Alexa and Laura, noting their troubled expressions.

"Come on, girls," she said. "Let's go see what's up."

They clambered into the car, and Nancie drove to Wren's place. She parked, and they made their way up the wooden front-porch stairs. Surprising them all, he met them at the door, swinging it wide, and beckoned them into the house.

"I thought you were dying," Nancie said somewhat facetiously as she walked in.

"Yeah, Dad, are you okay?" Alexa asked. "You didn't pick me up at Mrs. Baird's today."

"I know. I slept all afternoon and didn't wake up until I heard Risa at the door. She brought over some chicken soup. She said her Italian grandmother made it and that it's a sure cure for my chest cold."

"Is Risa here?" Nancie questioned softly yet warily. "Maybe I'd better go."

"No, it's all right. I wouldn't let Risa in because I don't want her to get sick." He reached over Nancie's shoulder and pushed the front door shut. "But since you've already been contaminated, you might as well come in and stay for supper."

"Very funny, Wren."

He smirked.

"I'm starved," Alexa said.

"Me, too, Daddy."

"Then come on in and sit down at the table," Wren invited.

"You sure?" Nancie hedged. "I hate to eat the meal Risa intended for you."

"I'll eat, too. . .and there's plenty." As they stepped into the dining room, Wren indicated the large red enamel tureen in the center of the table. "This would likely feed an army, wouldn't you say?"

Nancie took in the sight, observing the crusty Italian bread beside the pot of soup, and was suddenly reminded of the old adage about reaching a man's heart through his stomach. Risa certainly knew what she was doing.

The girls sat down at the table, and Wren headed for the kitchen to fetch some bowls and utensils. Nancie followed him.

"Here, let me do that. You're sick."

"I'm not that sick," Wren protested.

"Sick enough to miss work, and I don't think you've ever done that before."

"Yeah, well, there's a first time for everything, right?"

Nancie didn't reply, but studied her ex-husband thoughtfully. His complexion looked pasty.

"What did the doctor say?" she inquired further, pulling two glasses out of the cupboard.

"He said I have to rest all week, and he gave me a work excuse."

"Hmmm. . ." Nancie filled the glasses with milk before following Wren into the dining room.

He lifted the lid off the kettle, and the appetizing aroma from the soup filled the room. With everyone at the table, Wren prayed over the food before they began to eat. Nancie felt a bit guilty partaking of the meal, knowing Risa would doubtlessly like to see her choke on every last bite. But she quietly ate anyway, since she had to wait for Laura to finish supper before they could leave for home. Besides, she felt concerned for Wren. She wanted to help him out if she could; however, snippets of her last conversation with Risa flitted through her mind. "I wish you'd get out of Wren's life forever."

Guardedly, she looked over at Wren. Did he wish the same? Was he only being polite for the girls' sake?

Suddenly he pushed aside his half-empty bowl, plucked a paper napkin from its plastic holder, and wiped his mouth.

"You can't be full already," Nancie said.

He shrugged. "Guess I'm not as hungry as I thought." He looked miserable.

"Wren, go to bed. I'll stay with the girls tonight. We'll clean up the dishes and I'll help Alexa with her homework."

"Aw, Nancie, I can't ask you to do that."

"Then it's a good thing you didn't ask," she replied tartly, although she hoped the sweet smile she threw his way would communicate her earnestness to help him out.

Rising from the chair, she collected dishes and strode into the kitchen. As she rinsed their bowls, she heard him question the girls about school. They'd soon be out for the summer, and both Alexa and Laura were looking forward to a break from homework. Minutes later, Wren sauntered in.

"You really don't have to do this, you know," he said, coming to stand next to her at the sink.

"I know."

"But you're trying to even the score, right?"

Nancie shut off the faucet and looked at him. "What are you talking about?"

"I let you come up to the cabin last weekend, so now you feel obligated to wash my supper dishes."

"Is that what you think?" Nancie asked defensively. Then she quickly changed her tone. "Oh, I suppose I deserve it."

Wren didn't reply, but took hold of his pill bottle and shook out a capsule. He swallowed it down with cough syrup.

Nancie gaped at him. "I don't believe it."

"What?"

"What you just did. The Wren Nickelson I know would have accurately measured that medicine before taking it."

"I guess I feel too lousy to measure."

A sarcastic quip almost escaped her lips before Nancie thought better of it. Wren wasn't one of those guys who whined and complained. He didn't act like an invalid when he caught a common cold or the flu, and he abhorred being coddled. The fact that he admitted to feeling "lousy" spoke volumes.

"Look, I can stay with the girls for a while tonight if that will make things easier on you. Otherwise, I'll go home and scrub my kitchen floor."

An amused expression spread across his features. "Your life sounds as exciting as mine."

"Yeah, well, I'm working on it."

"Me, too."

Nancie took his arm and propelled him toward his room, but she couldn't squelch her sudden curiosity. "How are you working at it?"

"Praying about some things," he answered vaguely.

"About you and Risa?" she prodded.

He gave her a sideways glance and grinned meaningfully. "I'm pleading the Fifth on that one."

"You're cute, Wren," she shot back at him.

"And you never answered my question."

"I know," she replied sincerely. "Maybe when you're feeling better, we'll talk."

"It's a deal. So, are you sticking around a while?" he asked at his bedroom door.

"I said I would."

"Good," Wren stated on a weary-sounding sigh. "I don't think I can stand another minute." He stumbled to his bed and crawled beneath the covers.

Nancie frowned after him, feeling more than a tad concerned. Following him into the room, she laid her palm on his forehead. "You're burning up. When did you take something for your fever?"

"After I got back from the doctor's office."

With a shake of her head, she walked to the bathroom. Opening the mirrored medicine cabinet, she pulled down a bottle of tablets. Then she filled a glass with cold water from the kitchen tap and returned to Wren. She had to wake him in order to feed him the pills.

"Thanks," he murmured.

"Sure."

After studying him for several long moments, Nancie decided

he would be all right. She made her way back to the dining room, where she cleared the rest of the dishes off the table.

"Is Dad going to be okay?" Alexa called from the living room, where she and Laura sat watching television.

"I think so. If he rests he should be fine in no time."

"I'm going to make him something," Laura said, bouncing off the couch and breezing past Nancie. Reaching the wooden hutch, she opened one of the long bottom drawers and pulled out several sheets of construction paper and a narrow container of watercolors. "Dad always feels better when I paint him a picture."

Nancie smiled and reentered the kitchen. She washed the dishes and wiped down the counters. Having accomplished that task, she returned to the dining room, where Alexa sat at the table, math book open, and across from her Laura continued to create her masterpiece.

"Want some help?"

Alexa peered up at Nancie and shook her head. "I think I'm getting the hang of it."

"Good." Nancie watched as her daughter resumed her homework, marveling at the fact that Alexa didn't have to be threatened into completing it. An argument between them had frequently erupted over the topic of her school assignments.

"You know, Alexa," Nancie began carefully, "you and I have been getting along well lately."

"Yeah." She brought her gaze up, wearing a tentative smile. "But I still want to live with Dad, okay?"

Nancie swallowed her disappointment. "Sure. . .except I hardly get to see you these days."

"You saw me this weekend."

"Yes. But I only saw you a couple of times last week. I think we should make plans to spend time together. Maybe you can stay overnight with me on Saturday nights."

Alexa shook her head. "I have to help Dad and get ready for church on Sunday."

"You could get ready at my apartment."

She shrugged and looked back at her arithmetic book, and Nancie sensed a barrier starting to build between them. She'd have to discuss this matter with Wren. Obviously he carried more clout with their oldest daughter than she did.

"All right, Alexa. Let's just forget it for now."

"Hey, I gotta idea," Laura piped in. "Lex can stay with you on Saturdays, Mumma, and Risa can help Dad."

"I don't think so, Laura," the eleven-year-old shot back emphatically.

"Why not?"

"Because."

Nancie pursed her lips and observed the exchange curiously.

" 'Cause why, Lex?"

" 'Cause Risa isn't a Christian so Dad can't date her, and that's what Risa wants. She wants to go out with Dad. Like any moron can tell!"

"I'm not a moron." Laura looked at Nancie. "Mumma, Lex just called me a moron."

"No, she didn't. Alexa was simply making a general statement." She gave the older girl a pointed look. "I hope that's what you were doing. A good Christian doesn't call her little sister names."

"Sorry, Laura," she muttered, lowering her eyes to the math book once more.

"I forgive you," came the priestly reply.

For a while each child concentrated on the task before her. Then Laura looked up from her picture. "Mumma, do you like Risa?"

Nancie raised surprised brows. "Um. . .well, I don't know her," she said diplomatically, "so I guess I don't know."

"I think she's nice," Laura said, dabbing her paintbrush in the glass of murky water. "And sometimes. . .well, I wonder if she's going to be our new mom."

"Didn't you just hear what I said?" Alexa shouted at her.

"Risa can't be our new mom if she's not Christian!"

"She might become a Christian, and then she could," Laura hollered right back.

"Shut up!"

"That's enough, girls." Nancie put a stifling hand on Alexa's shoulder. "I think it's time to change the subject." Regardless of the words tumbling from her lips, Nancie's insides were churning. She glanced at Laura in disbelief. "But before we do, I want you both to understand that no matter what happens, I will always be your mother. Got it? There will never be a 'new mom' as long as I'm around."

"Does that mean you and Dad are getting back together?" Alexa asked. Hope pooled in her soft brown eyes, rendering Nancie momentarily speechless. "Mom?"

"I don't know what's going to happen," she finally replied in a whispered voice.

Alexa was thoughtful, then squirmed in her chair. "Mom? If you and Dad did get back together, would you have to get married all over again?"

Nancie frowned, thinking about it. Then she wagged her head, trying to clear it. She was actually thinking about it!

"Um, yeah, I guess we would," she mumbled.

"Well, if you did get married all over again," Alexa persisted, turning sideways in her chair so that her knees bumped against Nancie's, "could I be in the wedding?"

Nancie's jaw dropped.

"Me, too. I want to be in the wedding!"

Nancie started laughing. She couldn't help it. How in the world had she gotten herself embroiled in this silly conversation?

The girls began to giggle because she was laughing so hard.

"I think that's a 'yes,' " Laura teased.

"You guys are too much," Nancie told them.

"Is it a yes, Mom?" Alexa wanted to know, looking earnest again.

Nancie sighed. "Okay, yes. If the impossible should ever occur, then you and Laura can stand up in the wedding. How's that?"

Laura cheered and Alexa smirked.

"Guess what my Bible verse is this week, Mom?" she asked.

"What?"

"Matthew nineteen, verse twenty-six: 'Jesus looked at them and said, With man this is impossible, but with God all things are possible.' "

"Mmm. . ."

"See, Mumma? It's not impossible," Laura said, her small face brightening.

"But there is one other thing," Alexa added.

Nancie lifted expectant brows. "What's that?"

"Just like Risa, you gotta get saved."

"Well, I've got news for you," Nancie said, wondering why her heart was suddenly hammering. Was she really that excited to share the news? "I think I am saved. It happened this weekend—actually, yesterday on the ride home. I talked to God the whole way, and I know He heard me."

Alexa let the pencil fall from her fingers and stared at her in disbelief.

"It's true," Nancie said warmly. "For years I heard your father tell me about becoming a Christian, but I never saw my need for it. . .until this weekend."

"Cool," Laura said. "I'm saved, too. Now we'll both go to heaven."

Nancie smiled at her youngest, but felt a bit concerned for Alexa. She seemed to have gone into shock.

"Alexa?"

"Dad!" she shrieked, causing Nancie to startle. "Dad!" Jumping to her feet, she bolted for Wren's bedroom.

"Alexa, stop." Nancie ran after her, wondering what happened, what had gone wrong. "Alexa, don't wake him up!"

Too late.

"What's going on?" Wren's voice sounded foggy.

"Mom said she got saved!"

"Alexa, will you please calm down?!" Nancie grabbed her arm in irritation. "Leave your father alone. He's sick."

"What?" Wren reached for the lamp on the nightstand and turned the switch. Squinting from the sudden brightness, he glanced at the two of them.

"Mom said she got saved!" Alexa said again.

Wren's gaze shifted to Nancie for confirmation.

She nodded, then shrugged. Now she wasn't sure what took place. Perhaps she'd been mistaken. . . .

Wren sat up a little straighter. "Tell me all about it."

"When you're better," she said, feeling oddly embarrassed. "And Alexa is going to finish her homework before she gets punished."

"Yes, Mom," she said obediently. She bounced from the bedroom, laughing.

"I can tell she's just terrified of me," Nancie murmured. She rolled her eyes and looked back at Wren. "What are you grinning at?"

"You. Did you really get born again, Nancie?"

"I don't know," she said honestly. "I guess so."

Wren threw off the covers and got up. He was still in his clothes—jeans and a sweatshirt, rumpled as they were. "I feel much better."

"Fibber."

He grinned and took Nancie's elbow. "Let's go into the living room and you can fill me in on the details."

sixteen

Wren's thoughts were spinning—and it wasn't from the cough medicine. Two days had passed since Nancie announced her conversion to Christ, and Wren still couldn't get over it. He felt certain it was a sincere decision on her part, too, even though Nancie hadn't known quite how to articulate it.

He shook his head as the noonday sun streamed down on him where he sat out on the front porch of the duplex. After all those years of praying for her, Nancie had finally become a Christian. And to think that he'd almost given up hope.

Two of the upstairs neighbors came out their front door and bid Wren a "nice day." Then they walked in the direction of the bus stop. Wren decided he missed not walking his route when the weather was so good. A sure sign he was on the road to recovery. Well, tomorrow was Friday, and he would see the doctor again. No doubt he'd get the "all clear" and go back to work Monday.

Just then Risa pulled up in her car. After parking alongside the curb, she got out, waved, and headed for Wren. He almost felt like he had conjured her up, what with the way his thoughts had been rambling.

"Hi," she said, taking a seat beside him on the porch step. She was dressed in her post office blues and had her sunglasses perched on top of her head. "You look better."

"I feel better." Wren smiled. "What are you doing here?"

"Lunch break."

"Ah."

"I wanted to come over and check on you. I've tried calling the past two nights, but only got your voice mail. I was worried."

"Nancie's been staying with the girls in the evening so I

127

can rest, and she won't answer my phone. The girls are almost as bad. Each one thinks the other's going to get it."

Risa shook her head. "Just my luck."

The wind caught her long red curls, and Wren felt her hair brush against his shoulder before she pushed it back off her face. He discretely shifted his position and inched away.

"Risa, I've appreciated your friendship for the last six months more than I'll ever be able to express."

"Uh-oh, I can hear a 'but' coming."

He grinned at her remark and continued. "But things have changed between Nancie and me, and it really looks like we'll get back together."

Risa fell silent, staring out across the avenue. Finally, she looked at him without a trace of sadness in her eyes, only concern. "If that's how you feel, okay. I respect your decision. But, I hope you're not making a mistake." Her gaze narrowed in all seriousness. "Wren, did you ever think Nancie might want you back because she's jealous of my interest in you?"

"I've considered the possibility, yes."

"Consider it again. Once Nancie's got you, she'll hurt you a second time. She wants you wrapped around her little finger so you'll be available to bail her out of any inconvenience. I mean, look, Wren, something goes wrong in her life and she runs to you."

He shook his head. "That's not the case."

"Oh yeah? Well, when I called you chivalrous, she said that was 'boring.' When I cheered you on at the basketball game, she reprimanded me, saying I was inflating your ego."

"You do have that effect on me," Wren teased.

He laughed.

She didn't.

"Nancie doesn't say a nice word about you, Wren."

He cleared his throat. "Like I said, things have changed."

"You defend her. . . ." Risa expelled an exasperated breath.

Then she sat back, casually resting her elbows on the next step up. "I can't believe it."

Wren thoughtfully considered his hands, dangling between his knees. "You know, Risa, I believe in second chances. Second and third and fourth and fifth chances even. I believe we ought to forgive someone four hundred and ninety times, and that's just for the same offense."

"Your ex-wife has surely surpassed that number."

"I'm not keeping score. And that's my point."

She leaned forward. "You're such a special guy, and Nancie knows it. That's why she's determined to keep you—except she wants to keep you on a leash."

"I think I'm smart enough to sense it if that were really the case. No, Nancie is slowly changing her mind about a lot of things, and I'm one of them. She's a Christian now. She came out and told me so Monday night."

"Oh, right." Risa laughed sardonically. "Your ex must be desperate! But I've got to admit, she knows where to throw her punch. I mean, I could lie and say I'd had some terrific religious experience and that I'm a Christian, too. I know your faith is important to you, Wren. But I'd never use it as a means to further our relationship."

"I'm glad to hear it, but that's not what Nancie's doing, either."

Risa lifted her palms in surrender. "Okay, I give up." She turned to Wren, placing a hand on his shoulder and looking him squarely in the eye. "But when she hurts you again, I'll be waiting with open arms."

With that, she stood and bounded down the steps, making her way to her car.

Wren let her go.

≥•

Risa considered herself a professional woman, so she pushed aside her troubled thoughts of Wren and his ex-wife and conducted business as usual. But as she left work, she noticed dark clouds gathering in the west, and they seemed to mirror her frustrations.

If he could only see what that scheming woman is up to, she thought.

She drove to her home, located in the lower east side of the city, parked her car on the street, then walked to the building. The smell of precipitation hung in the air. More rain was coming, and, inevitably, more tears.

Inside her apartment, she set down her work bag and strode to her bedroom, where she changed clothes. Once she'd pulled on her jeans and a T-shirt, she heard the deep rumble of thunder and decided to watch the approaching storm from her living-room balcony.

I ought to talk to Wren's pastor, she brooded. *Maybe he could straighten Wren out. Counsel him. Perhaps the good reverend might even absolve Wren's marriage and convince him that God wants us all to be happy, not martyrs.*

After a moment's deliberation, she stepped back into the apartment. Yes, that's what she'd do. She'd drive over to Wren's church and see if the pastor was there. Last Thursday night, the guy was playing basketball with the other men. There was a chance he'd be there tonight.

Grabbing her purse off the glass-topped table, Risa hurried to her car. She climbed in only seconds before the sky opened and released its pent-up fury.

Was it some sort of sign from heaven?

When Risa was a child, she might have thought so. She used to believe God's emotions were synonymous with the weather reports. When He was angry, there would be thunder and lightning. If God was happy, the sun shone brightly. During the winter months, except at Christmastime, of course, God deserted all of Wisconsin and the temperature plummeted.

Risa smiled inwardly as she drove slowly through the storm. How utterly silly. Obviously, God left human beings to their own devices. If He really cared what happened here on earth, He would have intervened on her behalf years ago. A loving, caring God would have sent a bolt out of the blue to strike her stepfather dead for all the physical and verbal abuse she'd suffered by his alcoholic hand.

Reaching the church, Risa shook off the shadows from her past and made a run for the side door. It was open, so she slipped inside. Finding herself in a hallway, she silently walked past the gymnasium. The lights were off. She wondered if she were the only one in the building, and it gave her an eerie feeling to think that might be the case.

Wandering down one corridor, then another, she found a row of offices. All but one was locked up tight. Seeing two men and a woman huddled around a copy machine, she cleared her throat.

" 'Scuse me."

They all turned her way and smiled a greeting.

"I'm looking for the pastor of this church."

"He's out of town until late Saturday," replied the petite woman. Her hair was a sandy brown and she wore a simple light blue skirt and white blouse.

"Okay. Thanks anyway," Risa replied, spinning on her heel.

"Hey, wait. Don't I know you?"

Chuckles emanated from the group.

"You know everyone, Mike," someone quipped.

With her hand on the doorknob, Risa glanced back and saw the familiar face of Wren's friend, Mike Gerardi.

Slowly she faced him and he stepped toward her.

"Risa, isn't it?"

"Yes." She tipped her head in polite regard. He sure wasn't dressed for a basketball game, what with his French blue dress shirt and neatly pleated khakis.

"Is there anything I can help you with?" he asked. "I'm one of the associate pastors here."

"You?" Risa was hard-pressed not to gape at the man. He

didn't look like a pastor. He looked like an ordinary guy. But then again, the pastor had looked just like everyone else out on the court last week, shooting hoops with the best of them. Odd how she had always thought clergy should be garbed in white robes and black collars—or was it the other way around? "Well, um. . ."

"We could go get some coffee and talk. Have you eaten dinner?" Mike snapped his fingers before Risa could utter a reply. "I got it, we can go to my cousin's place. Best Sicilian food in town. We can talk there."

Typical Italian man, she thought as he ushered her from the office. And she supposed that if she didn't mention any names and voiced her concerns in a hypothetical manner, it might be all right. On the other hand, if Mike was indeed one of Wren's buddies, perhaps he'd be the perfect candidate to talk some sense into him.

They strode through the hallway side by side.

"Are you married?" she asked. She always asked.

Mike stopped short. "Are you kidding? I wouldn't be taking you to dinner if I was married."

"Sorry. It's happened before."

An understanding expression flittered across his dark features.

"I'm not married, either," she said.

"I know." Mike resumed their stroll to the parking lot. "Wren told me."

This time Risa braked. "He did?" She eyed him suspiciously. "What else did he say?"

Mike grinned. "What, you expect me to talk on an empty stomach?"

With a sigh of mild annoyance, Risa allowed him to take her elbow and escort her out of the building. They jogged through the rain to his car, where an almost startling notion entered her mind. . . .

Nana would adore Mike Gerardi.

seventeen

The storm passed and now a light drizzle fell beyond the kitchen window as Nancie helped Wren clean up the supper dishes. She washed; he dried and put them away. Since it was after nine, both girls were in bed, sleeping. Laura had begged to stay overnight, so Nancie acquiesced. Wren was feeling much better, and the task of getting both his daughters up, fed, and off to school wouldn't be a strain.

Nancie smiled coyly. "Do any writing with all your time off this week?" she asked. "I mean, now that you're up and around. . . ."

He grinned back at her. "As I matter of fact, I puttered around a little this afternoon."

She rinsed a glass and set it in the drainer. She couldn't wait to read it. Maybe she should confess to peeking at his manuscript. . . .

"Say, Nancie, I've been meaning to bring up this subject for a while," Wren began, changing the direction of her thoughts.

"What subject?"

"You and me."

"Oh."

Lifting his brows, Wren regarded her speculatively. "Oh?"

Nancie laughed softly. "I guess I've been expecting it."

He nodded thoughtfully. "So what do you think?"

"I think," she hedged, shutting the faucet off and turning to face him, "that part of me wants very much to reconcile, but the other part is scared silly."

Wren smiled patiently. "I think that's normal, don't you?"

"I suppose."

He flipped the dish towel over his shoulder and his expression became one of earnestness. "What frightens you about our getting back together?"

Nancie knew the answer. She'd lain awake several nights this week, contemplating this very topic. "I'm afraid that we might find out nothing has really changed between us."

"But it already has."

"Somewhat. But, to be totally truthful, I'm afraid you're going to hold me back."

"In what way?" he asked, wearing a puzzled frown.

"In my career, my education."

Wren inhaled deeply, and Nancie wondered if he were trying to keep his temper in check. Now that the religious barrier between them had toppled, this was the great divide that still existed. "Have I ever stood in your way, Nancie?"

"Not physically, no. But you have emotionally. Throughout our marriage, you wanted me to be someone I'm not. You wanted me to be a Ruth Baird. . .not that there's anything wrong with her. But that's not me."

"Excuse me, Nancie, but I distinctly recall a reversed scenario. You're the one who wasn't satisfied with me or anything I gave you. You wanted some Fortune 500 executive and I'm just a plain ol' mail carrier."

She held up a forestalling hand. "I know, I know. That's true. And I'm sorry I hurt you. I'm sorry for the awful things I said and did."

Wren reached out and stroked her cheek compassionately. "Forget it."

"But you were just as awful."

He dropped his hand and sighed. "I failed as a husband. Okay. I admit it."

"But you've got to understand why you failed, Wren, or else it's going to happen again."

"I failed because I couldn't afford a BMW and vacations to Paris."

"Wrong. You failed because you could never accept me for who I was, faults and all. After Alexa was born, you wanted me home—cooking, cleaning, changing diapers—but I wanted a part-time job to stimulate my mind."

"And you got it."

"But not without a fight and a host of complaints. Then, after Laura came along, you pressured me to become a Christian, emphasizing that the Bible says women should be kept at home."

He frowned. "The Bible doesn't say that."

She pointed an accusatory finger at him. "You showed me the very passage."

Wren shook his head. "You misinterpreted it, Nancie. The Bible doesn't mean women should be physically kept at home, like some prisoner. It refers to an attitude. And can I help it if I want a home complete with wife and kids? I think that's a basic need, not some lofty expectation."

Nancie folded her arms and raised a stubborn chin. "I'm not giving up my career."

"And I don't want you to. I'm simply asking that you love me, the girls, and our home more than your career and education."

"But I do. I always did."

Wren shook his head. "No, career and education took first place in your heart, Nancie, to the point where you were frantic about finding someone to stay with our children when they had chicken pox instead of caring for them yourself. They were sick. They needed their mother. But instead, you paid a stranger to come into our home and baby-sit."

"She was very qualified."

"Doesn't matter." Wren irritably raked his fingers through his hair. "As a wife and mother your family takes precedence over your job or anything else."

"See, there you go," Nancie retorted. "You think you're putting me in my place by using that bossy, arrogant tone of yours. Listen, Wren, when it comes to sick kids, you can take off your share of work to stay home and baby-sit, too."

He shook his head. "As a mother, that's your responsibility."

Nancie lifted a brow. "Not when I earn more money than you do."

The verbal blow hit its mark; she could tell from Wren's wounded expression. Instantly she felt bad for hurling the fact in his face.

He pulled the dish towel off his shoulder and gazed out the window above the sink. "This isn't going to work. I can tell already."

"Maybe if you'd compromise, it could."

Wren shook his head ruefully. "That's not it." He glanced at her briefly before looking back at the rain-splattered pane. "You'll cringe when I say this, but a man's home is his castle."

Nancie groaned and, yes, cringed.

"Look, as dumb as it sounds, it's true. I've got to lead my family, Nancie. I can't surrender my God-given responsibility to you."

"Why do you have to surrender? Why do you have to be king? Can't we have a democracy?"

Wren glanced at her once more, obviously considering the questions.

"There's got to be some way we can work this out," she said. "I'm willing, if you are. But you can't be so dogmatic about traditional family roles. Times have changed."

"God hasn't. He's the same yesterday, today, and forever."

Nancie threw her hands in the air. "Here we go again."

"And for your information," Wren continued, "I've done all the compromising I can ever do. As my spouse, you can work and go to school, but you have to be a wife and mother first."

"That's a male chauvinistic view if I ever heard one."

"Whatever. That's my final offer. Take it or leave it."

"Offer?" Nancie laughed bitterly. "You can take that offer

and stuff it in your ear, Wren Nickelson!"

She turned on her heel and stomped to the living room, where she grabbed her purse. Nearing the front door, she picked up her coat and umbrella before storming out of the house.

๕

Wren felt horrible for losing his patience with Nancie. She was a new babe in Christ, but he'd acted as though God's standards should automatically make perfect sense to her. Why couldn't he have lovingly, calmly vowed to work things out and then let the Lord nurture Nancie so she'd form her own convictions about her role as a wife and mother?

He knew the answer. Pride. And pain. Nancie had hurt him with her salary barb, and he'd reacted. Just like always.

The phone jangled and Wren scurried to find the cordless receiver, hoping the caller was Nancie.

To his disappointment and delight, it was his mother.

"Hi, Mom, how are you today?"

"Well, my arthritis flared up with all this rain, but otherwise, I'm fine."

"Good." Wren collapsed onto the couch and put his feet on the coffee table.

"What about you? That chest cold clear up?

"Just about."

"Good. Well, I won't keep you. I'm just calling because I was talking to Ron Dempsey this morning. He's a friend of Dad's and is going to be retiring soon. He's in charge of the mail room at that company. . .oh, I forget its name, but it's the one that practically owns the whole town. The printing company up here in Neenah."

"American Printworks."

"That's the one!" his mother declared. "Ron told me they've been interviewing for his replacement, but can't seem to find the right person. I mentioned that you've worked for the United States Postal Service for over ten years, and Ron said you should apply."

"Why?" Wren asked, unsure of where his mother was going with this idea.

"Why? Well, because. . .you'd be closer to us."

He chuckled.

"The cost of living is lower up here, Wren. And the air is cleaner. Besides, Ron said this job would probably pay more than what you're making as a mailman, and the company offers excellent benefits."

"Hmm. . ." Wren thought it over, then shrugged. He wasn't looking to change jobs. "Thanks for thinking of me, Mom, but—"

"I told Ron that you've been sick all week but felt better now, except you still had the day off. He wanted me to tell you to call him and he'd fit you in for an interview this afternoon."

Wren started to protest, then realized this could be an answer to his prayers. He had already decided it wasn't smart to work at the postal station with Risa. Wren knew he had to transfer, for her sake as much as his own. There could never be anything between them. As for a wage increase, that would please Nancie; however, he wondered what she'd say about moving up north. An instant later, Wren knew she'd refuse to leave her career for him.

If she really loves you, she'll follow you anywhere, his heart of hearts seemed to say.

But that's exactly what he was afraid of—that Nancie didn't love him quite that much.

Then perhaps it's time I found out.

"Wren?"

He snapped from his soul-searching. "Sure, Mom, give me that phone number. I'll call right away."

eighteen

Wren steered his way through rush-hour traffic, glad that he didn't have to do it every day. Between all the construction and the road rage, it was a harrowing business just trying to change lanes.

Nevertheless, the trip to Neenah had been worth it. He'd filled out an application in the human resources department, had an interview an hour later, had gone to his folks' place for a while, then returned to American Printworks for a second interview with Ron Dempsey, the current manager of the mail room and distribution center. Wren had the feeling he would be offered the position. Of course, company officials wanted to verify employment and check references; however, they said they'd get back to him Monday morning. Everyone involved had seemed pleased and optimistic.

Now if only Nancie would see his possible job change as a blessing—that is, assuming she hadn't entirely changed her mind after last night.

He continued along the highway, mulling over every detail of his life these past few weeks. The miraculous had occurred; Nancie had become a Christian and was considering a reconciliation. It still seemed so impossible—but that was God, accomplishing the improbable, the incomprehensible. Nancie's salvation had definitely strengthened Wren's faith. And each evening this past week, he'd had a small taste of what it would be like to have his family back together. He wanted it so badly, but realized now he couldn't push or run ahead of the Lord. On the other hand, it was sheer torture to be so close to the very thing he had hoped and prayed for, yet he was still so distant. However, he had a hunch this employment development would be the deciding factor. Wren had been praying earnestly since his mother's phone call this morning and felt strongly that if offered the manager position, he would accept it.

Whether Nancie liked it or not.

The traffic inched its way along the interstate, and Wren realized that he typically made decisions in an effort to please Nancie, not God, and certainly not himself. He wanted her love and would do just about anything to get it. Certainly there wasn't much give and take, although Wren saw changes. But would they last?

They will if I start behaving like more of a man and less of a wimp. Wren had to chuckle. George was definitely beginning to rub off on him.

☙

Risa wrapped up some last-minute end-of-day details before gathering her belongings.

"Whatcha doing this weekend, Risa?" a coworker asked, closing the customer window before balancing her drawer.

"Not sure yet."

"No hot dates?"

Risa gave the brunette a hooded glance. "Yeah, right." In truth, she wished she did have a "hot date." She wished Wren would forget his ex-wife. . . . She wished so many things. Unfortunately, her dreams weren't likely to materialize. She'd heard much the same thing about religion, the Bible, and God's expectations from Mike Gerardi as she did from Wren. Since the two men were friends, they were obviously in cahoots. But who would have ever guessed Mike was a pastor? Not Risa, that's for sure. And as much as she hated to admit it, he'd shown her a nice time last night.

My family would drop over dead if they knew I'd gone to dinner with a pastor, she thought amusedly. Except it probably wouldn't happen again.

Bidding her subordinates a good weekend, Risa locked up the postal station and walked to her car. She had hoped Wren

would be back at work today, but he'd called late this morning to say his doctor's appointment had been changed to
Monday morning. Deciding to take a bit of a detour on the
way home, she stopped at his place to say hello. Maybe they
could order a pizza and rent a movie. Wren's kids would like
that. And if that witch of an ex-wife was there. . .

Risa shoved the idea aside. She didn't want to think
about it.

She pressed on the doorbell, peeking through the front-door
window. The flat appeared deserted. . .sounded deserted, too.
She rang the bell once again. Nothing.

Disappointed, Risa turned, stepped off the porch, and
made her way home.

❧

Nancie looked at her watch when the phone rang. Lifting the
portable off the coffee table, she checked the Caller ID. "It's
about time, Wren," she answered. "It's almost seven o'clock."

"Hi. Yeah, sorry." He coughed, but it sounded one hundred
times better than five days ago. "Ruth said you've got the girls."

"They're here. Where have you been?"

"In Neenah."

Nancie frowned. "Visiting your parents?"

"I did that, too," he said, sounding irritatingly vague.

"What else did you do?" she probed, unable to keep the
trace of sarcasm from her voice.

"I had a job interview."

Sitting up quickly, Nancie almost dropped the phone. "A
what?"

"An interview. At American Printworks."

"I see. . . ." Nancie chewed the corner of her lower lip,
wondering why he didn't say something about an interview
before now.

"It was an impromptu thing," he stated, as if divining her
thoughts. "How come you picked up the girls at four o'clock?"

"I left work early and stopped by your duplex. I wanted to

talk to you. When I didn't find you home, I went to Ruth's. That's when she told me you were going to be late, so I figured I might as well take the girls to my place and feed them."

"Thanks."

"Did you pay Ruth?"

A pause. "Yep."

"Good." Nancie reclined on the couch again. "The girls are at the playground with their bikes. Alexa's girlfriend is with them."

"Okay. Well, when should I pick them up?"

"Can you come right now, Wren, so we can talk while they're gone?"

"Sure. I'll be right over."

Nancie clicked off the phone. She didn't think Wren sounded like himself. He sounded stiff, unemotional. Oh, well, he either wasn't feeling well or he probably thought she was still angry about last night—and she had been. But she'd gotten over it. And she knew Wren didn't stay mad for long. Must be the job interview thing causing him to act guarded.

American Printworks. Nancie knew of the company. Who didn't? It was a large, prestigious firm, one that touted its small express airline that only the elite could afford. Moreover, rumor had it that in order to get hired at AP, one had to "know" someone, another employee. But of course, that wouldn't be ethical, let alone legal. However, she believed there was some truth to the report.

So whom did Wren know? And why had he applied there? What if he got the job? Would he move up north or commute an hour and a half each way to and from Milwaukee? A job up in Neenah? What's he thinking?

Ten minutes later her intercom alerted her to Wren's visit. Her questions were about to be answered. She buzzed him up and met him at the doorway of her apartment.

"Tell me about this job interview," she said, beckoning him inside. As he walked in, she gave his attire a once-over, noticing Wren still wore navy dress pants, a crisp, light blue cotton shirt, and coordinating but loosened necktie.

"First things first," Wren replied. He regarded her with a soft, rueful expression. "Sorry about last night."

"Apology accepted."

He nodded a reply, but Nancie sensed he still felt troubled.

"I'm sorry, too," she stated out of obligation more than anything else.

A hint of a smile curved Wren's mouth. "I think you were right to admit being afraid last night. It'd be horrible to wind up divorcing a second time. The girls would be devastated."

Nancie folded her arms and looked at him askance. "What's your point, Wren?" she asked tartly. "Have you suddenly changed your mind?"

"No. . .no, I haven't. But we've got a ways to go yet, don't we?"

She felt confused. "Is that why you're considering a job transfer to Neenah?"

"Partly."

She shook her head. "How's that going to mend things between us?"

"Well, for one, the position is a step up and I'd get a wage increase. . . ."

Nancie immediately understood. "You're still upset with me because I threw in the remark about making more money."

"I'm not upset, but yeah, it bothers me."

She shook her blond head. "Look, Wren, get out of the dark ages. Women in today's society can be the primary breadwinners."

"Maybe so. But not in my family."

Nancie brought her chin back up and glared at him. But to her amazement, he didn't back down. He stared right back. Finally, it was she who tore her gaze from his.

Walking to a living-room window, she looked out over the

housetops. She could see the playground in the distance and recognized her daughters' colorful T-shirts near the large wooden gym set. She glanced at her watch. The girls still had twenty minutes before they were supposed to be home. Nancie had given them a curfew of eight o'clock, since it stayed light outside until about 8:30.

Satisfied that Alexa and Laura were safe, she turned back to Wren. He'd taken a seat on the couch, and Nancie saw the weary etchings around his eyes. No doubt today had exhausted him since he hadn't yet completely recovered from his bout of bronchitis. He should have stayed home and rested instead of traipsing up north.

"Okay, so let's pretend you get this job," Nancie began. "Then what? Are you planning to commute?"

"No, I'd have to find a place up there."

She nibbled her lip in contemplation. "So, I'd have the kids during the week and you'd come down on Friday night, pick them up, and take them back to Neenah with you for the weekend?"

He sort of nodded and shrugged simultaneously. "We'd work something out."

Sure we would, she thought sarcastically. She could well imagine the fight Alexa was going to put up. She'd want to live in Neenah with Wren. Nancie would never see her. And what about day care arrangements when she had to travel?

"Wren, if you're so far away, what am I supposed to do if I have an out-of-town conference or meeting to attend?"

"You'd have to see if Ruth can watch the girls overnight, I imagine."

"And you'll pick up the tab for that?"

Wren shook his head. "No. In fact, I decided that I'm not forking out money for day care expenses anymore."

"Excuse me? I thought you said you'd be making more money."

"I did, and I would. But then you'd get more support out of

my paycheck, so you can pay the baby-sitter."

"Oh, no, that's your responsibility."

"No, it's not. Check our divorce decree, Nancie. I'm required to pay you a percentage of my income. It's says nothing about day care costs."

Nancie narrowed her gaze at him, realizing what he was up to. "You're trying to back me into a corner and force me to conform to some simpering wifely role, aren't you? Well, forget it. It won't work. Fine. I'll pay the day care fees."

"Good. You can start next week."

She glowered at him. "You're despicable. I can't believe I considered remarrying you." She put her hand across her forehead, feeling a throbbing headache coming on. "It's all coming back to me now—the whole reason I divorced you in the first place."

Wren stood, his shoulders slumped slightly forward as if a tremendous load bore down on them. Still Nancie refused to feel guilty for hurting him. He was hurting her right back.

"I want a wife and a mother for my daughters," he said so quietly that she had to strain to hear him. "I don't care if she works outside the home or goes to school as long as the girls and I are always more important than her career and her education. And, Nancie, if you're not willing to leave a job for me, that tells me I'm not as important."

"Oh, Wren, give me a break." She felt like a lead weight was lodged in her chest. "You might give a girl a little fore-warning, you know. You might ask and not dictate."

"Would you?" he questioned, appearing almost hopeful. He closed the distance between them and slipped his arms around her waist. "Would you leave your position at a prominent firm to be my wife and live two hours north of here? We could buy a cute little home in the country. . . ."

Nancie felt sick. This past week she'd concluded that she would never in her life find a man who loved her as much as Wren did. But was love enough to compensate for the sacrifices he was demanding of her?

He kissed the side of her head and folded her into a snug embrace. She hated to admit she needed him, but, weakness in her character that it was, she did. She was the kite flying gloriously in the air. He was the one down below, holding onto the string. If he let go, she would twirl uncontrollably and crash to earth. But now he was reeling her in!

Loosening his embrace, he took a small step backward. He searched her face. "I'm sorry about playing hardball here tonight. I'm not trying to trap you into a decision or force you into doing anything you don't want to do. But I wanted to be sure you understood my feelings because, as you said, you might not be able to live with them."

Nancie felt like crying, but pride held her tears in check. "I guess I have a lot of thinking to do," she replied more confidently than she really felt.

Wren nodded before leaning forward and placing a light kiss on her lips. Then he smiled into her eyes, although it was the saddest smile Nancie had ever seen.

"I'll pick up the girls at the playground," he announced, making his way to the door. "Have a good weekend."

"Thanks. Same to you."

They sounded all too formal.

She watched him go and, after the silence in the lonely apartment filled her ears, a sort of numbness filled her heart. Had Wren just let go of the kite string?

nineteen

Nancie slept fitfully and awoke early on Sunday. It seemed as if her internal alarm clock refused to let her snooze past seven no matter how much or how little sleep she'd gotten the night before. Rising and making a pot of coffee, Nancie actually considered attending a worship service; however, she didn't have the nerve to walk into Wren's church. She'd snubbed members of that congregation for years, and she didn't see how she could show up unannounced. They'd probably stone her.

Retrieving the fat newspaper from the hallway, Nancie sat down on the couch, coffee in hand, and picked through each section disinterestedly. Finally her conscience was so riddled with guilt that she closed her eyes in prayer.

"God," she murmured, "I'm sorry I was rude to those people. I said terrible things to them in the past, and if I ever get an opportunity, I'll apologize. I promise."

Feeling somewhat better, she drew her attention back to the newspaper. However, try as she might, she couldn't concentrate on a single article. Instead, she became preoccupied with memories, flitting unbidden through her mind. And for some odd reason, she recalled every unkind thing she'd ever said to Wren.

"God, it's me again," Nancie whispered, gazing at the stark white ceiling in her living room. "Okay, I'll admit it. I have a problem of foaming at the mouth when I get angry. I say things I don't mean. I've hurt Wren in the past, too, but he's not exactly perfect, either, You know."

With an exasperated sigh, Nancie pushed the newspaper off her lap. With all this confessing, she might as well go to church.

But she wouldn't. She couldn't. Unless. . .

Getting up from the couch, she found the cordless phone and dialed Wren's number. No answer. She glanced at the clock on the wall. Surely he hadn't left for church already. Chewing her lip in thought, she wondered if he'd taken the girls up north to visit his folks. With all this new job business on his mind, Nancie had a hunch that was the case.

"God, please don't let Wren get this job," she pleaded, squeezing her eyes shut. "How are we supposed to renew our relationship if he moves out of town?"

She plunked down in a nearby armchair, frustrated, agitated. She'd gotten in on the ground floor of a career with endless possibilities. Once she completed college, she was practically guaranteed a promotion. And Wren expected her to walk away from such an opportunity?

It was then that she heard God speaking to her. Not in an audible voice; rather, it was more an impression on her heart, like an inscribing in stone. "You wanted to reprioritize. Here's your chance."

Immediately Nancie recalled how last Tuesday she had mourned the direction of her life. She had all but convinced herself that Wren was in love with Risa, but such wasn't the case. Then all week long, she'd felt married to Wren in all but the physical sense. It had been like a delightful game of playing house.

But could she really find happiness in a "wifely" role for the rest of her life?

Ruth Baird came to mind, so Nancie decided to call her. It was an impulse, no doubt about it. However, she knew Ruth and her husband attended another church in town. Perhaps she'd sit in on its pastor's sermon this morning.

"Oh, sure," Ruth said cheerfully after Nancie explained the situation. "We'd love for you to join us this morning."

Ruth listed the address and time of service.

"Great. I'll see you soon."

Nancie hung up the phone, then hurried off to shower and dress.

≈

Risa placed one wary foot in front of the other and stepped into the sanctuary of the modest little church. She hadn't been to mass in years and hadn't ever gone to a Protestant "worship service" as Mike called it. Slipping into one of the back pews, Risa still couldn't believe the guy was a pastor—and a most convincing one at that. Even Wren hadn't been able to get her out to church.

Wren. Her heart still ached miserably just thinking about him, although she knew it was her own fault. He never led her on, but she'd forged ahead anyway. She was only too glad that he wasn't here today. She didn't want Wren to think she'd begun stalking him, for pity's sake! But Mike had assured her Wren was out of town for the weekend. Several unanswered telephone calls seemed to confirm it.

At last the service started, and the congregation was asked to open their hymnals. Organ and piano music filled the small church, and soon the singing matched it in a joyous sound. Next came some announcements, followed by the offering, and then the pastor stood at the pulpit and began his message. At the end of the service, she went away thinking about what she'd just heard. It was much the same thing Wren had showed her from the Bible the night of the rainstorm.

As she made her way into the throng heading out of the sanctuary, Mike approached her and pulled her aside. "So what did you think?" he asked.

She smiled tersely. "I think this religion stuff isn't for me."

His dark brows furrowed in concern. "Well, let's talk about it. My sister, Patti, wanted me to invite you for a noon dinner. She's a great cook and—"

"No thanks," Risa cut in. She couldn't be certain of the good pastor's intentions. Was he after another convert or looking for romance? In either case, she wasn't interested. "Have a nice life, Mike."

With that, Risa left the church, fully expecting never to set foot inside the place again.

❧

Nancie felt a little guilty watching Ruth load her dishwasher and straighten up the kitchen while she just sat there doing nothing. "Are you sure I can't help you?"

"Positive."

"Well, I appreciate you inviting me over for lunch."

"It was fun."

Nancie smiled, although it was bittersweet. "All the commotion around the table made me miss my girls."

"Oh, I'm sorry," Ruth said in a sympathetic tone. "It's got to be hard being away from them every weekend."

Nancie nodded. "And it's getting harder."

Ruth turned and leaned her backside against the counter. Tipping her light brown head to one side, she gave Nancie a thoughtful look. "What do you want most in your life right now?" she asked. "If you could have anything in the world— any one thing—what would it be?"

Nancie couldn't help showing a little smirk. "A million dollars and my fam—"

"Ah!" Ruth held up a forestalling hand. "I said any one thing. You said money."

"Oh, now, wait a minute. Before you think I'm a 'material girl,' you need to know I was only kidding around."

"Were you?"

"Of course."

"Jesus said, 'Out of the abundance of the heart, the mouth speaks.' "

Nancie merely smiled at the comment, but inwardly she bristled and hoped she wasn't about to hear a second sermon today.

"You know, my sister has a great job. I used to be so envious of her. All I could see was that she got to drop off her kids at day care and then go to her challenging work while I was stuck at home changing diapers and listening to whining, bickering children all day."

Nancie gave her a curious look. "You? You felt that way?"

"Uh-huh."

"That's how I felt. Exactly."

"Well, then my sister's six-month-old daughter died of SIDS—sudden infant death syndrome. She'd been napping at the sitter's house at the time. It wasn't anyone's fault, of course, but my sister blamed herself—still does."

"How tragic."

Ruth agreed. "But through that misfortune, I realized how precious every day is with my kids. I vowed never to take them, my husband, or my home for granted again." She chuckled. "God supplied my heart with an abundance of love and then He blessed me with my own business—a day care."

While Ruth turned back to the sink and finished cleaning up, Nancie thought about little Nathan's drowning on Memorial Day. Yes, life was precious. And yes, Nancie had taken her family for granted, too. However, she wanted to make things right. But how could she accomplish it if Wren moved out of town?

He just can't get that job, she thought with an edge of determination.

Sometime later, she left the Bairds' home and drove back to her apartment, where she changed clothes. Then she lay down in her bedroom and took a short rest. All the while she pleaded with God to foil Wren's possible employment with American Printworks. She found it ironic, too, that she was actually praying he wouldn't make the move, take the step up. Years ago she would have been rejoicing. Then again, years ago she didn't have her career in the sales department to be concerned with.

Why do I have to be the one to make the sacrifice? she wondered. *That's not fair.*

But soon Nancie pushed aside the question and prayed once more that she wouldn't be forced to give up anything— because Wren wasn't going to get that job!

⌘

It was seven o'clock when Wren finally phoned Nancie and let her know he and the girls were back in town. He offered to drive Laura to her place, but Nancie said she'd pick her up instead.

On the drive over, Nancie rehearsed what she wanted to tell Wren. She wanted to say she loved him and that some-how, some way, they'd work everything out.

Nancie parked her car and walked to the house. Crossing the porch, she pressed the bell switch. Alexa appeared and threw open the door, mumbling a brief, "Hi, Mom," before dashing off to whatever she had been doing. Nancie let her-self in and, as she shrugged out of her spring jacket, she saw the girls were involved in some electronic table tennis game that they were playing using the television and two hand-held controls.

"Where's your dad?"

"In the kitchen," Alexa replied, "with Risa."

Nancie's heart stalled. "Oh, really?"

At the sound of her sharp tone, both girls glanced at her. She gave them each a tight smile, then proceeded to the kitchen. She could hear Wren talking, although she couldn't make out what he was saying. But it didn't matter. That woman had to go.

Pausing in the dining room, Nancie collected her wits. She took a deep breath and tried to remember her new resolution to watch her words, to hold her tongue.

Then she walked in.

"Hi." She looked at Risa, then Wren, noting his mild look of surprise.

"Did you just get here?" he asked.

"Just now. I rang the doorbell and everything."

Wren momentarily pursed his lips in thought. "Oh," he said as realization struck, "I was in the basement."

Nancie shifted her gaze to Risa, who glared back at her. Nancie couldn't deny that the redhead made a fetching sight in her fitted jeans and white cotton top. Her curly hair hung around her face and shoulders attractively, and it caused a painful swell of jealousy in Nancie's chest.

"What are you doing here?"

A sad but smug grin tugged at Risa's glossy mouth. "I came to say hello to a good friend and make sure he's feeling better."

"And she's just leaving," Wren cut in before Nancie could utter a reply.

He ushered Risa toward the door, and Nancie watched until the woman was gone.

"I suppose you're in your prime having two women fighting over you," she shot out as Wren strode toward her.

He stopped short under the wide wooden door frame between the living and dining rooms. Nancie sensed a battle brewing between them.

"Mom, don't be mad," Alexa said, dropping the game control and bolting up off the floor. "I let Risa in while Dad was in the basement doing laundry." She looked from one parent to the other. "I didn't really think about it. I just let her in. Sorry."

Wren's features softened. "It's okay, sweetheart," he told her. Looking back at Nancie, he pointed to the kitchen, where they could verbally tear each other to pieces without the girls overhearing.

Spinning on her heel, Nancie marched into the other room. She chose a place to stand, then turned to face Wren and folded her arms in front of her. She hated feeling so jealous and suspicious; however, Alexa's admission had alleviated much of it.

"Do you see why I can't stay in my present job situation much longer?" Wren began.

"Risa's that much of a temptation, huh?"

"You'd better believe it."

"Wren, that's so weak. Can't you stand up to her? Tell her to get lost!"

He shook his head and lifted his gaze as if to say she didn't understand. And she didn't.

"Nancie, I care about Risa. That's the truth. . .and the problem. She was a good friend to me when I needed one. But she knows I want to reconcile with you and she's hurt by it. I always made it clear to Risa that ours was a platonic relationship, but, regrettably, things between us somehow developed more than I should have allowed."

Nancie tipped her head. "What does that mean?"

Wren sniffed and gazed at the linoleum flooring. "It means I used Risa for months the same way you used me on Memorial Day weekend. I say that to my shame." His gaze came back to hers. "But she filled a void."

"Okay. . ." Nancie's anger dissipated. "That's understandable."

"It's unfortunate."

"But now it's over, right?"

Wren shook his head. "It'll never be over, Nancie, as long as Risa makes herself available to me."

"Because you care about her?" Nancie questioned carefully.

Wren nodded.

"Are you telling me you're in love with her?" Fingers of apprehension climbed her spine as she waited for the reply.

"No, I'm not telling you that." He rubbed the back of his neck wearily.

She narrowed her gaze in disappointment. "But you're not denying it."

Wren dropped his hands and gave her a level look. "No, I

guess I'm not completely denying it, either, although I don't know what it is I actually feel for Risa. I know it's not a relationship God would want me to pursue, but these feelings are real and they're there and I don't know what to do with them."

Nancie mulled it over. "Well, at least you're honest."

Without a reply, Wren exited the kitchen and Nancie listened as he instructed Alexa to get ready for bed. When the girl reached the hallway, Nancie watched her do a silly jig while singing about her last two and a half days of school.

Wren reentered the kitchen minutes later, and out of the corner of her eye, Nancie saw Laura scoot to her bedroom.

"Laura wants to sleep over," Wren informed her, "and I thought that might be okay. When the girls go to bed, we can talk some more."

Nancie nodded, seeing the wisdom in that. "Can I make a pot of coffee?"

"Go for it."

Stepping to the cupboard, she pulled out the coffee can and began preparing the brew. She marveled at Wren's predicament, yet understood very well how it had come about. He was handsome and sensitive to a fault. The all-around nice guy. And yet if he hadn't been so "nice," Nancie might still be wallowing in that horrid depression. . .or worse, she might be dead.

One at a time, the girls came out to say good night and kiss their mother. Again, that feeling of playing house enveloped her, and she noticed Alexa and Laura were cherishing each and every aspect of the game.

But was it just pretend? Nancie had to decide. Could she give Wren what he wanted in life and still be happy, or was he better off with Risa?

No way! her heart protested. *She can't have him.* Nancie grinned. That answered that.

Once the coffee finished brewing, Nancie poured a cup

and headed for the living room. She discovered Wren sitting on the couch, hunched forward, his hands folded and suspended between his knees. She thought he looked discouraged.

Compassion filled her being and she sat down beside him. Setting her mug on the coffee table, she slipped her arm across his shoulders. "I love you," she whispered. "I'm not just saying that, either."

She watched him grin, although his gaze remained fixed on his hands.

"The truth is," she continued, "I never stopped loving you, Wren. But for years, I loved myself more."

Taking a deep breath, he sat back and Nancie let her arm fall away.

"I love you, too. I know that's for sure."

Smiling, she reached for her coffee and tucked her legs under her before she curled up beside him. Wren brought his arm around her.

"I'll make you forget all about Risa," she promised. "Everything will work out."

"You think so?" There was a challenging glint in his eyes that Nancie found irresistible.

"I know so." She kissed him to emphasize her point.

"Mmm. . .maybe you're right."

She laughed. "And I didn't even spill my coffee."

His grin broadened. But after several moments, his somber look returned. He searched her face. "Do you love me enough to follow me anywhere, Nancie?"

She knew he was referring to his possible job offer with American Printworks. "I love you enough to discuss it if it comes down to that."

But it wouldn't, she thought. *It just couldn't!*

twenty

It was ten o'clock in the morning, and Nancie felt as though she were walking on air, above the clouds. Her boss had named her to head up their department's next big project. At last she could prove herself and earn the respect of the company's top executives. What a way to start a Monday!

The rest of the day continued in much the same vein. Over and over again Nancie thanked the Lord for her good fortune, certain that this was God's way of letting her know Wren hadn't gotten the job and that she wouldn't have to ditch her career. They could still remarry and begin anew—Wren need only transfer to a different postal station.

Around 4:30 that afternoon Nancie phoned him, knowing he would likely be home. As it rang, she wondered if he was feeling bummed out; she warned herself to be sensitive.

Then he answered.

"Hi. Did you just walk in?" she asked.

"About twenty minutes ago. I've got Laura with me."

"Okay." A nervous swell rose in the pit of her stomach. "So, what's the verdict?"

A pause. "I got the job. You're talking to the new manager of American Printworks' mail room and distribution center. I handed in my resignation today."

Nancie could scarcely believe it. She had prayed so hard. . . how could God have allowed this to happen?

"Nancie? You still there?"

"Yes, I'm here." She swallowed hard. "I've got good news, too," she said, although the glory of it had suddenly vanished. "I'm in charge of the sales department's next project.

It's a big one."

"Congratulations." He sounded sincere.

"Yeah, same to you," she felt obligated to reply.

"Should we celebrate? Name the restaurant."

She was so overcome with disappointment, she could barely croak out an answer. Finally she told him to choose the restaurant.

"Okay. I'm sure the girls and I can think up a place to go."

"Do they know?"

"About my job change?"

"Yes."

"I just finished telling them before you called, but they've got a lot of questions. Maybe we can field them together at dinner."

"Sure," she said. "Sure, that'll be fine."

With that, she hung up the telephone and felt her heart sink.

❧

Wren could tell Nancie wasn't happy about his new position. He knew she wouldn't be. But he had to hand it to her, she was doing a great job in keeping her displeasure from the girls.

"So are you guys getting married?" Alexa wanted to know.

Wren forked a piece of steak into his mouth, leaving Nancie to answer that one. She appeared quite dignified, sitting across the table from him. Her hair was pinned up in a professional manner, and the beige and navy plaid suit she wore incorporated tiny gold stripes that enhanced her elegance.

Nancie caught his gaze and held it. "I don't know. We're trying to work things out."

Wren decided that's the best reply he could hope for at this point.

"Until you do," Alexa said, "can I live with Dad?"

Wren turned his attention to his baked potato. He wanted

to let Nancie respond to as many of the girls' questions as possible, since they were the same ones he'd been pondering all weekend. When he had tried to discuss them with her before, she had changed the subject each time he brought it up.

"If you live with your father," Nancie replied, "I'll never get to see you."

"Yeah. And besides, it's not fair," Laura interjected, "because I wanna live with Dad, too."

He tried not to wince, although he had a feeling that was coming.

"Wren?" He looked up, noting Nancie's pained expression. "Any suggestions?"

He set down his fork. "Well, perhaps for the summer the girls can live with me during the week. Mom said she'd baby-sit for free. On Friday nights I can drive them to your place."

Nancie drove her knife into her veal with a bit more force than necessary. "See, girls? Your dad has it all figured out." She shot him a look that could have withered a cactus.

"Are you mad, Mom?" Alexa asked perceptively.

"Not at you, sweetheart," Nancie crooned.

"At me?" Laura wondered with a worried frown.

"No, honey."

The girls turned wide eyes toward Wren.

"Your mom doesn't like it that I have to move so far away for my new job," he tried to explain.

Alexa smiled impishly and looked at Nancie. "Are you going to miss him?"

"Incredibly."

Wren had to grin at Nancie's underlying sarcasm. But later, it wouldn't be so funny. He had a feeling he was in for it.

Alexa didn't pick up on the quip, however. "Well, that's dumb, Mom. Why don't you just marry Dad and move, too? Then we'll be all together and no one will have to miss anyone."

"Sounds like a plan to me," Wren said. As long as he was in trouble, he might as well dig himself in deep.

"I think I'm ready for dessert," Nancie announced in a velveteen voice as she pushed her plate aside. "And I'm in the mood for a huge hot fudge sundae."

Alexa and Laura were in immediate agreement, and Wren said nothing. He knew better than to interfere with women and their chocolate.

ॐ

Risa managed to avoid Wren for an entire week and a half. He had candidly informed her that he loved his ex-wife and planned to remarry her, so Risa stayed out of his way. When their paths did happen to cross, she was polite, friendly, and unemotional. She gave him her best supervisor smiles and words of encouragement, but never let on how badly her heart ached. Never once. For such a performance, Risa decided she ought to get nominated for an Academy Award. However, on this particular Wednesday afternoon, she couldn't seem to mind her own business. She'd been secretly observing him all along and recognized misery when she saw it.

She sneaked up on him as he prepared to leave for the day. "Excuse me."

He whirled around. "Hey, Risa," he said casually.

"Hey." She leaned up against the wall and folded her arms. "Pardon me for noticing, but in spite of your exciting new job and wedding plans, you don't seem very happy."

"Yeah, well, Nancie and I are barely speaking to each other." He caught himself and shook his head. "Never mind. Forget I said that."

"Too late, it's already said." He made like he didn't hear her, so Risa shrugged. "Okay. Well, you know my phone number if you ever feel like talking."

"I almost called a couple of times," he confessed in hushed tones. "But I can hardly go running to you every time my wife gets mad at me."

"Ex-wife," she corrected him. "And this only goes to show that you'd be wise not to make the same mistake twice."

Wren expelled a weary-sounding breath and, as usual, Risa's heart went out to him.

"So what are you two sparring about now?"

"Nancie can't bring herself to leave her career in order to marry me and move to Neenah."

"Surprise, surprise."

Wren lifted a brow, indicating his displeasure at the cynicism.

"Sorry. But if the man I loved asked me to leave my job and marry him, I'd have my written notice on the boss's desk in five minutes." Risa shoved her hands into her uniform pants pockets and stared down the corridor. "True love is hard to find."

He didn't reply.

"Want to go find something to eat after work and talk?"

"No, but thanks for the offer." He gave her a grateful smile.

She shrugged again. "Okay. Guess I'll see you tomorrow."

"Yeah—see you tomorrow, Risa."

She walked away, amazed at Wren's faithfulness to a woman who deserved nothing but his condemnation. *Why can't it be me?* she wondered ruefully. *Why can't it be me?* She had a hunch it never would be her, either, because she'd never again in her life meet another Wren Nickelson.

❧

Nancie felt sick to her stomach as she and the girls carried boxes out to the rented truck. He was really doing this, the scoundrel. He was forcing her to choose between him and her career. Well, despite what he wanted, namely, a conversation on the subject, Nancie refused and kept a tight lid on her emotions. No doubt that's what was really getting to Wren. Her silence was killing him. However, she took no delight in the revelation. It was killing her, too.

"Hi, Nancie. Nice to see you again."

She gave the dark-haired man standing on the porch beside Wren a perfunctory smile. He looked vaguely familiar.

"This is Pastor Mike Gerardi from church," Wren informed her.

"Oh, right. Hello." She walked past him and suddenly remembered her promise to God. Hadn't she said she'd apologize for her rudeness in the years gone by if she ever got the chance?

Yes, she had, and now it was time to make good on that vow. God was the only one she shared her heart with lately. But for days she had felt like the Lord had let her down, had abandoned her. Then last week, clearly out of the blue, Ruth Baird made a comment, likening God to any good parent. "He doesn't give us everything we want just because we ask for it." Nancie had understood the parallel at once, but it still didn't make her decision any easier.

"Um, Mike? Can I have a word with you?"

He looked surprised, but nodded.

Nancie ignored the curious frown on Wren's face and waved the pastor into the rapidly emptying dining room.

"What can I do for you?" he asked.

She inhaled deeply, gathering her resolve. Apologies didn't come easily. "I just wanted to tell you how sorry I am for being rude in the past. I know you and other members of your congregation only had my best interests in mind whenever you came calling, but I didn't see it that way."

He smiled. "All's forgiven."

"Thanks."

Nancie returned to the girls' bedroom and began packing another box.

It was around the dinner hour when Nancie decided to take a break and sit on the covered porch. The four guys from church who had come to help with the furniture had long since gone home, while Wren and the girls went to pick up a pizza.

Lowering her bone-tired body onto a step, she surveyed the discarded junk, piled along the curb. A light drizzle had begun, and if it wasn't trash before, it would be soon. Strangely enough, she felt remorse at the sight of the worn couch and matching armchair, the scuffed-up side tables, coffee table, and boxes of chipped dishes and cracked goblets that Wren said he no longer wanted. Completely understandable, and yet those were the same things, in the same sorry shape, that he insisted upon salvaging when Nancie had filed for divorce almost two years ago.

Wren had changed.

With elbows on knees, Nancie rested her head in her hands. And that's when she saw it. The electric typewriter. It was protruding at an odd angle from one of the cardboard boxes near the street. Inexorably, she felt drawn to it. She walked off the porch and into the light rain, wondering why Wren had pitched his typewriter. Didn't he need it until he bought a computer?

Nancie lifted the heavy, clunky machine from the box and, to her horror, she found scraps of Wren's novel, wet and crumpled yet recognizable, lying beneath it.

"But you can't throw it away," she murmured. "You haven't finished the story."

Her heart dropped as she considered the implication. Because of her, Wren's dreams were all but dashed at the roadside. She stood there for a moment, feeling like she couldn't breathe.

Then suddenly she knew what she had to do. Lowering the typewriter back into the box, she dragged it across the street and stowed it in the trunk of her car. When at last the deed was done, Nancie rubbed her palms together and made her way back to the duplex.

twenty-one

Warm, early-morning sunshine spilled down on Nancie as she sat on Wren's front porch. Make that Wren's former front porch. He had left Saturday night in the rented moving truck filled with his belongings. Alexa and Laura had gone with him, and all three were now temporarily staying with Wren's folks. Since he was to start in his new position next week, Wren had informed Nancie that he planned to use these next few days to clean up the old place and get his security deposit back, then find an apartment in or around Neenah. Nancie had taken it upon herself to help Wren with both projects, and now she sat awaiting his arrival.

She smiled, anticipating his expression. He would wonder why she wasn't at work; after all, it was Monday. And then she'd tell him.

Carefully, Nancie pulled the folded piece of paper out of her blue-jeans pocket and stared at the information. She'd been busy yesterday, and she'd been a real estate agent's nightmare. Without Wren knowing, she had driven up north, bought a local paper, and spent all afternoon scouting through homes that were listed on the market. She knew exactly what she wanted, and she was stubborn enough not to settle for anything less, in spite of the best sales tactics. But she might have found it—their castle in the clouds. She and Wren had an appointment to tour the home this afternoon. From what the real estate agent said, it sounded perfect.

Now all she had to do was tell Wren about it—about everything.

Tucking the note back into her pocket, Nancie waited another half-hour before Wren finally showed up. As she had

164

expected, he was surprised to see her.

"What are you doing here?" he asked, stepping slowly to the porch. He wore an old blue T-shirt and worn-out, paint-splattered jeans; he carried a plastic bucket in his left hand.

"I thought I'd help you clean the flat."

He raised curious brows. "Well, thanks. Did you take the day off or something?"

Nancie nodded.

"That's nice of you."

She followed him into the empty, hardwood-floor echo-chamber of a house. "Actually, Wren. . .I resigned this morning. I gave my boss a two-week notice and then I took today off."

He turned around slowly and faced her. If he'd been surprised before, he was dumbfounded now. His dark brown gaze fastened to hers, as if trying to read into her heart, to guess her motives.

But that wasn't necessary. Not anymore. From now on, she'd be transparent with Wren.

"I love you," she stated simply. "I can't live without you. I mean, even after the divorce, when I thought I was independent and on my own, I still relied on you for a lot of things. But you were kind enough to be there for me despite the way I hurt you." She smiled, though tears filled her eyes. "Sorry, buster, but I know a good thing when I see it." She strode forward, pointing her index finger at him. "You're not getting away from me, and I'm never going to let another woman come between us. Got it?"

He nodded and slipped his arms around her waist. "You're the one I love, Nancie. Always have, always will."

"I know," she said in complete honesty. "And I love you that much more for it."

He pressed a tender kiss against her lips, sealing their precious new commitment. Then he held her against him, and Nancie lay her cheek against his shoulder.

"I'll never hurt you again," she promised.

He kissed her forehead in reply.

She lifted her head. "No more arguing, fussing, fighting. . . none of it. We're going to live happily ever after."

Wren smiled into her eyes, before releasing her almost abruptly. "That's music to my ears, Nancie, but first things first and that means a wedding."

"I promised the girls they could be in it."

Wren gaped at her for a moment. "When did you do that?"

"A couple of weeks ago."

"Was someone planning to inform the groom of these plans?"

Nancie laughed. "Eventually. But you've got it easy. All you have to do is show up in a tux."

Wren pursed his lips agreeably. "I think I can handle that."

"And. . .you might have to pay for the reception," she added on a note of chagrin.

"I can handle that, too, as long as you don't rent the Taj Mahal or something."

Smiling, she leaned forward and grabbed the handle of the wash bucket. "It's a deal. But in the meantime, we've got a busy day ahead of us. We have to get this place cleaned up in time to make a three o'clock appointment."

"What appointment?"

Nancie nibbled her lower lip somewhat nervously. "I can't tell you just yet. Is that all right?"

After a brief deliberation and a curious, if not doubtful, look, he nodded.

By eleven-thirty the place was spotless. By noon the landlord showed up, inspected it, and wrote Wren a check for his security deposit. Next, Nancie followed Wren in her car as they drove to his parents' house, where they changed clothes. His parents, along with Alexa and Laura, were full of questions. Wren and Nancie promised to answer them after they returned.

Hand-in-hand, they walked to the driveway.

"I'll drive," Nancie said, "seeing as I have a vague idea of where I'm going."

"A vague idea?"

She had to laugh at Wren's concerned expression; however, her insides were trembling. This was going to be the tough part. But restoring dreams usually wasn't easy.

She pulled the slip of paper from her pocket and reread the directions. "I did a bit of homework yesterday," she began, "and I might have found us a place to live."

"That's the big secret?"

"It's part of it."

For once in her life Nancie felt grateful that Wren was a patient man. He didn't drill her or quiz her, but sat quietly in the passenger seat, awaiting his fate.

Finally, she realized they were nearing the house, so she pulled off onto the shoulder of the road. They got out of the car and started walking. To their right, a brown, wood-plank fence marked off the property.

"I haven't seen this place yet, but from the description I was given, it sounds like what I want."

Wren inclined his head somewhat hesitantly.

And then they came upon it—a two-story brick house on a hill. In the front, off to one side, was a miniature turret that gave the place a castlelike appearance.

Nancie laughed. "It's perfect!"

Wren put his arms on the fence and stared at the structure.

She cleared her throat. "A man's home is his castle."

He glanced at her with amusement in his eyes.

"A castle in the clouds," she added.

Wren didn't respond to the use of his novel's title. Then again, Nancie wasn't supposed to know the name of it.

"Can't you just see George and Nan trying to redecorate this place without killing each other?"

That did it.

Slowly he turned, one hand on his hip, the other on the fence. He gave her an incredulous look. "How do you know about George and Nan and the castle?"

Nancie swallowed and did her best to appear contrite. "I found your book."

"Found?"

"Accidentally on purpose. You see, it was at about the time I felt sure you were trying to get custody of the girls, so when I saw you stuff some papers in the buffet drawer and lock it, I got suspicious. I thought they were legal documents. I also watched where you put the key. After you left for your writing class, I peeked in the drawer. . .and found your story."

He said nothing, but his dark eyes and stony expression spoke volumes.

"Don't be angry with me, Wren," she pleaded. "I like your book. You're a wonderful writer."

He shook his head and turned away, gazing in the direction of the house again. "I never intended for anyone else to see that story. I'm so embarrassed."

"Don't be. I'm the only other person who knows about it. And I'm not going to push the issue, but I hope you're going to continue writing your book."

"Hadn't planned on it."

"But I have to know how it ends."

"Happily ever after," he quipped.

Nancie backed up to the low fence and rested her elbows on it. "Well, I certainly hope George told Lucia to take a swim in the moat with the alligators."

Wren chuckled and moaned simultaneously. "Oh, Nancie, I can't believe you read that piece of tripe!"

"Don't call it that." She shrugged, unable to fully explain how she felt. "Your story affected me. . .and I think it affected you, too."

"It was good therapy for me to write those scenes," he

admitted. "They saw me through a lonely, discouraged time in my life. But I'm not really a writer."

"Yes, you are. Okay, so you're not exactly Faulkner or Hemingway. Not yet, anyway. But you've got a special way of conveying a meaningful message. . .and it changed my life."

"Well, that just proves God can use anything."

She smiled and let the subject go. Then she nodded toward the house. "What do you think?"

"I think we can't afford it, by the looks of it. What's the asking price?" When she told him, his tone changed. "That's more than reasonable—it's downright inexpensive. What's the catch?"

"The owner got transferred out of state and wants a quick sale. What's more, it's an older home, kind of in the middle of nowhere, and it's not part of the fashionable subdivision we passed, so it's not as desirable as some of the other homes on the market."

Wren seemed contemplative.

"Should we at least take a look?" she prodded.

"Sure, why not?"

They walked up the inclined driveway and met the real estate agent in the yard. After briefing them on several particulars, he led them into the vacant house.

They toured the first floor—living room with a fireplace and sunroom, formal dining room, spacious kitchen, family room with patio doors leading outside to a deck. Upstairs there were three spacious bedrooms and one smaller room that the agent said had been a sewing room.

Nancie nudged Wren with her elbow. "This can be your writing room."

"Yeah, right."

"Well, feel free to wander," the agent said. "I'll be downstairs. When you're through with your inspection, we can talk."

"So, what's your opinion of the place?" she asked, once the real estate agent was out of earshot.

He gazed out the window. "It's a pretty small castle and not half as spooky as the one in Saxony."

Nancie smiled.

"It's also more costly than the half-dollar George had to pay."

"I'm glad you mentioned money," she said, coming to stand beside him. She looped her arm around his. "I have a certificate of deposit that I bought after I sold our house in Shorewood. I planned to pay for my education with it, but I'd rather we use it for a down payment instead."

Wren turned from the window and eyed her speculatively. "You sure about that?"

"Positive."

"That's quite a sacrifice."

"Not really. Not when I consider the whole picture of our lives together with our daughters." She smiled up at Wren, knowing she meant every word.

He stared back at her thoughtfully. "We need to pray about buying this house, Nancie."

"All right," she replied easily, although there was a time when that directive would have irked her to no end.

"But I like it." His gaze went back to the window and beyond. "I like it a lot. I guess we can at least put an offer in on it."

Nancie's spirit soared. "And this will be your writing room? And you'll finish the rest of the story?"

"Yes, I'll finish it." Wren looked back at her, smiling broadly. Then he gathered Nancie in his arms. "But you know, we really don't need fairy tales in order to live happily ever after. We've got the Lord, each other, and two beautiful daughters. That's enough."

He kissed her then, and Nancie knew without a shadow of a doubt that what he said was true.

epilogue

Wren never thought he'd see the day. Today marked his first book signing, and he felt almost as nervous as when he and Nancie remarried.

With his wife at his side, he sat in front of a rectangular table draped with a charcoal gray cloth. It matched the cover of his book, *Castle in the Clouds,* and the manager of this particular Christian bookstore had been kind enough to host Wren's first autograph session.

Now, if only a few readers would show up. . .

"Don't be nervous," Nancie said, deciphering his thoughts. She sat calmly beside him in her denim jumper, looking every bit of eight months pregnant. Still, she gave him a reassuring smile. "It's a good book. It's going to be a best-seller."

Wren had his doubts. However, the fact that his novel had even been published was triumph enough for him. And he couldn't have done it without Nancie.

One by one, readers straggled to the table, looked over Wren's novel, and chatted a bit. Occasionally someone actually bought his book and returned for an autograph.

"This isn't exactly the kind of book signing I imagined," he confided to Nancie. "I envisioned a line extending out the door and into the mall—and writer's cramp. But it's eleven-thirty, and we've sold all of three or four copies."

"That's because your book is so new. It takes time to build a readership."

Wren sighed. "I'm glad you're my PR person. And I'm doubly glad you work for free!"

Nancie's amber brown eyes twinkled with amusement. But then a little frown began to mar her brows.

"What's the matter?" Wren followed her line of vision and saw a woman with a headful of tangerine curls peering thoughtfully at a shelf in the store's Christian Living section. Tucked in the crook of her arm was Wren's book, and he didn't have to see her face to know the woman was none other than Risa Vitalis.

He glanced back at Nancie, deciding she ought to feel secure enough in their relationship not to be jealous or threatened by Risa's presence.

Her next words confirmed his hunch.

"I've been thinking about her lately," Nancie said of Risa. "I've been praying for her." She met his gaze. "I hope that, like your character Lucia, she finds the Lord."

Wren nodded. The more the plot had thickened in his novel, the less he had liked the idea of killing off that particular antagonist. Besides, his research had shown that probably wouldn't have been well-received in the Christian marketplace.

"Here she comes," Nancie whispered.

Wren turned and watched Risa's approach. She smiled a greeting before handing him his book.

"I heard about your book signing from Mike Gerardi. Congratulations. . ."—she glanced from Wren to Nancie—". . .both of you."

"Thanks," Wren said, picking up his pen. He felt flattered that Risa would make the ninety-minute drive to Appleton from Milwaukee in order to support his latest endeavor.

"How have you been?" Nancie asked.

"All right. I see you're expecting child number three."

Wren looked at Nancie in time to see her lovingly pat her protruding belly in affirmation. Feeling like the proud papa that he was, he grinned and handed the book to Risa.

"I'm glad to see you guys are doing okay," she said with a light of sincerity in her eyes. She looked at Wren. "Good-bye."

It sounded final. It looked final.

Risa swung around and left the bookstore.

"I hope *she's* doing okay," Nancie murmured, her voice tinged with concern.

Wren expelled a slow breath. "If Pastor Mike is keeping in touch with her, I'm sure she's just fine."

Nancie smirked. "Now wouldn't that be a story?"

"What, Risa and Mike?"

She nodded, raising a conspiratorial brow. "Definite possibilities, wouldn't you say?"

He shrugged; he hadn't really thought about it, although they did seem an unlikely pair. "Well, one thing I've learned over the course of the past eighteen months is that all things are possible with God."

"Amen to that!"

Wren and Nancie shared a chuckle, and then another reader stepped up to the table. A smile lingering on his face, Wren reached for the book the man held out to him. *Amen to that,* Wren silently agreed as his smile widened to an ear-to-ear grin.

M·O·N·T·A·N·A

Montanans are legendary for their courage and willingness to take on challenges as big as the Montana sky. But the heroines in these four inspirational novels are ordinary people facing mountains of trouble. As the comforts of daily routine are threatened, they'll need to dig deep for a sustaining faith.

Set in the fictional town of Rocky Bluff, Montana, the four complete contemporary novels by author Ann Be demonstrate the power of prayer, friendship, and love.

paperback, 464 pages, 5 ³/₁₆" x 8"

❤ • ❤ • ❤ • ❤ • ❤ • ❤ • ❤ • ❤ • ❤ • ❤

❤ • ❤ • ❤ • ❤ • ❤ • ❤ • ❤ • ❤ • ❤ • ❤

A Letter To Our Readers

Dear Reader:

In order that we might better contribute to your reading enjoyment, we would appreciate your taking a few minutes to respond to the following questions. We welcome your comments and read each form and letter we receive. When completed, please return to the following:

Rebecca Germany, Fiction Editor
Heartsong Presents
PO Box 719
Uhrichsville, Ohio 44683

1. Did you enjoy reading *Castle in the Clouds?*
   ☐ Very much. I would like to see more books
      by this author!
   ☐ Moderately
      I would have enjoyed it more if _____

      _____

      _____

2. Are you a member of **Heartsong Presents**? Yes ☐ No ☐
   If no, where did you purchase this book?_____

   _____

3. How would you rate, on a scale from 1 (poor) to 5 (superior), the cover design?_____

4. On a scale from 1 (poor) to 10 (superior), please rate the following elements.

   _____ Heroine   _____ Plot

   _____ Hero   _____ Inspirational theme

   _____ Setting   _____ Secondary characters

5. These characters were special because_____

_____

_____

6. How has this book inspired your life?_____

_____

_____

7. What settings would you like to see covered in future
   Heartsong Presents books?_____

_____

_____

8. What are some inspirational themes you would like to see
   treated in future books?_____

_____

_____

9. Would you be interested in reading other **Heartsong
   Presents** titles?   Yes ❏   No ❏

10. Please check your age range:
    ❏ Under 18   ❏ 18-24   ❏ 25-34
    ❏ 35-45   ❏ 46-55   ❏ Over 55

11. How many hours per week do you read?_____

Name _____

Occupation _____

Address _____

City _____ State _____ Zip _____